Book Two of The Revelation Trilogy

Fallen Angel

Matt Eastwood

Printed in Australia
First Printing, 2019
ISBN: 978-0-6485929-4-5
White Light Publishing
Melton, VIC, Australia 3337
www.whitelightpublishing.com.au

For my son,
Benjamin Timothy Eastwood

ACKNOWLEDGEMENTS

There are only three people I want to acknowledge for this book. During the editing process, I came across certain moments within my writings that brought me to tears. I remember writing them, and the pain it took to put my grief into words was absolutely overwhelming. I lost my brother, and in writing and editing this book, I found a sense of closure. I will always miss you Tim, and I hope this trilogy does justice to serve your memory well. You were unbeatable, fearless, and loyal. Everything combined to make up the awesome power that is Marcus, you emanated every day. I will forever try to live up to that.

My son Benji challenges me every day. You may think it coincidence that one of the main characters is named Ben. Which came first? Although I started writing the book before he was born, I always knew he would come into my life. He is my heart, my soul, and I couldn't imagine my life without him. It is such a beautiful feeling watching him grow, and to be able to teach him this crazy roller coaster existence we call life. Becoming a father to this amazing, sweet and sometimes challenging little boy, is by far the greatest thing that I have ever achieved.

And, to my fiancé, Lena. Words can't describe how you have changed my life. Yes, there have been times - and I'm sure we will face many more - where we were thrown curve balls. Sometimes, many at once. The strength that we possess together is one of the greatest feelings I have known. With you by my side, I am invincible. Bring on the terrible; I'll walk through Hell. We've moved mountains, so what could possibly stop us? Together we can accomplish anything, and every day, the beautiful person you are inside and out, just makes me love you more and more.

I am so blessed to have, or have had, these people in my life. I will always cherish them.

THE REVELATION

The great sword was removed from battle for a greater purpose. When the time comes, the angel to which the sword is bound will have to search for his sword and reclaim it. Once he has reclaimed his sword, he will then assume the position he was chosen to fulfill, and a great alliance will be formed.

The angel will fall, and rise again with the great power that he was destined to behold. The most powerful sword must belong to the most powerful angel. The sword will strike the great stone and all the lost angels will rise up into the sky, and then the angel will reunite Heaven with its lost souls and begin the battle to fight for the good of the Heavens and the Earth.

To which an angel will be born of human blood and live as a human until the angel inside of him is set free. His identity will be found by the colour of his wings, for he will be a Seraph. The human angel will lead the armies of Heaven to victory. The sword will spill human blood and merge the two pieces, which will then harm its possessor, leading us to defeat the bringer of all evil. This revelation will be confirmed by the one true God.

PROLOGUE

Dorian ran, holding his right side as his blood oozed from under his hand. He had been shot, but this was no ordinary gunshot wound. As an ordinary bullet would have no effect, these bullets were specifically designed to harm his kind. He rushed quickly as he was chased by his pursuer through the roughest part of town. Derelict buildings surrounded them, closed down shops, and burnt down or demolished rubble. Dorian found an open doorway and darted through it, as a hallway stood in front of him with doors leading off of it; two on the left, one on the right. He decided not to go into the first room, as that would be the first room his pursuer would check, nor the second. He figured if he went into the third room, he would hear his enemy check the other rooms first. He rushed into the third room, which was the second door on the left, and quietly closed the door behind him. He rummaged around in the darkness, looking for something to help with his wound. He hadn't ever bled before; this was a new feeling for him. Then again, he had never been on the receiving end of this particular enemy. He was rarely in a position that he could be harmed, since most others always feared him. He felt defeated, and for the first time in his life, he was afraid.

The rain battered against the building and the wind howled through the open door, which made it very difficult for him to listen as he held his wound. The pain was unbearable, and even though it made it hard to concentrate, he heard a sound. A faint footstep on the floorboards near the front door. He slowed his breathing as much as possible and strained to pick up any other faint sound, bending his neck, as if it would somehow outstretch his ear more. He heard nothing. He held his breath, believing that a single exhale would alert his enemy, even against the sound of the rain and the wind. Although, he had once heard that this individual was a born hunter, and could hear a pin drop. The door burst open. Marcus stood there with a long coat, over a button up shirt, and bootleg pants over a pair of black boots. He had a large black revolver in his hand, a Colt Dragoon. It was a very old black powder pistol, with a silver cross on the grip. Black powder pistols packed more punch than your conventional six shooter, and Marcus looked after his Dragoons well. Marcus raised the gun and shot Dorian again in his left shoulder, which thrust Dorian back against the wall with the sheer power of the bullet. He began bleeding more.

"Blessed bullets," he said, "clever."

Marcus stepped closer as the gun disappeared from his hand. Dorian lunged himself at Marcus despite his wounds and began to attack him, throwing heavy roundhouse punches. Marcus deflected each blow with precision and speed, noticing Dorian was leaving himself wide open in the middle. He blocked a heavy left and lunged forward with his right fist, knocking Dorian down. Dorian came back with even more ferocity as Marcus knocked him down again, and again, and again. Eventually, Dorian stayed down.

"Where is Lucas?" Marcus asked.

Dorian took a deep breath and groaned in agony. "That, my friend, is a secret."

"I'm not your fucking friend."

Marcus stepped even closer and grabbed Dorian by the collar of his jacket. A dagger appeared in Marcus' hand. His trusty blade.

"You can't have him," Dorian said.

"He came from my blood, thanks you to. He's an abomination, and needs to die. Just like you need to die."

"You kill me, you'll never find him."

Marcus narrowed his eyes. "Seems you won't tell me anyway. So there's not much use keeping you."

The room around them began to change as Marcus transported the two of them to Purgatory. Grey sludge flowed around them as the smell of death and decay befouled their nostrils. They quickly caught the attention of others nearby, with only one thought on their now vacant minds: fresh meat.

A horde of hungry humanoid figures began to advance on them, as Dorian began to smirk with a small sense of hope. Marcus checked his surroundings and noticed they were about to be attacked. His blue wings shot up out of his shoulders as the looming crowd stepped back. Anger filled Dorian's' eyes as he began to change shape. His body started growing larger as the human-like skin stretched and tore. It was like watching a creature shed a cocoon, but much more gruesome. Horns began to grow all over his head and body as his scaly brown skin emerged from his human form. Plate metal armour covered his large devilish chest. After the transformation, he stood over Marcus, who was still holding onto the now torn empty jacket with one hand, with his dagger in the other. Dorian let out a mighty roar as Marcus dropped the jacket and shot himself forward with his dagger in his left hand, below the knuckles, towards his elbow. His right hand firmly held the handle as he plunged the dagger toward the giant beast, trying to strike in between the plates of armour. He missed as Dorian grabbed Marcus in his oversized clawed hand and pulled him closer with a sense of victory. Marcus stabbed him in his exposed shoulder which caused Dorian to let out a mighty roar in pain, leaving his mouth open. Marcus saw his chance as his Colt Dragoon appeared instantly in his hand and stuck it directly in Dorian's open mouth. He pulled the trigger.

Dorian's eyes opened wide in panic as he realised his error. He then began to erupt in a fireball of flames, and Marcus fell to the wet cement-like ground that plagued Purgatory. He stood up and looked at his body covered in the sludge and then noticed he was still surrounded by hungry mouths, as embers fell around them from Dorian's fiery demise. They didn't advance on Marcus any further. Their vacant minds stirred a memory. They remembered who he was.

They didn't engage him.

Marcus disappeared.

CHAPTER 1

42 years later...

The hooded figure quickly ran towards Ben. His footsteps were silent as he got closer. He pushed Ben in the back and Ben fell onto his hands and knees. He rolled over and saw nothing behind him. He pulled himself up onto his knees just as a tiny demon came rushing out of the shadows in front of him. It was about two feet tall and had large black eyes and big pointy sharp teeth. It swiped at him as he shifted backwards from his knees and onto his hands behind him. He began shuffling backwards towards a wall.

"Hello bird boy!" the tiny demon said.

Ben noticed more demons behind the little one, and they were a lot bigger than the little one. From where Ben was on the ground, he could see four of them, and they all looked to be about six feet tall. The hooded figure came up behind them. He looked quite small compared to the demons around him. He was maybe an inch or two shorter, and looked fairly thin. "Grab him," the hooded figure said.

Ben pressed his back as close to the wall as it would go. He had no idea what was going on, and he didn't particularly like the situation he was currently in. A drop of sweat trickled down his forehead as the four demons began moving around him; two on his left, and two on his right. The tiny demon in front of him stood very still, trying to look intimidating. It was working. Ben looked up to see the hooded figure wasn't there anymore. The small demon moved closer to Ben. It started snapping and snarling. It looked like a baby demon. Ben almost wanted to touch it, but thought it would be best if he didn't. He tried to edge closer to the wall, but he was as far back as he could go. At that moment, a sharp blade began coming out through the tiny demons stomach. The demon gasped in pain and tried to look around it to see what was behind it. It started to panic. Ben looked up and saw Marcus with the Sword of the Angels piercing through the small demon. The sword was so far through the demon's stomach that it was almost touching Ben.

"Sorry I'm late," Marcus said.

The four demons surrounding Ben turned their focus onto Marcus and the two closest to him stepped forward. Marcus lifted his sword up with the small demon still on it. It was amazingly, still alive. One of the closer demons lunged at Marcus. He sidestepped and stabbed it through the stomach. The tiny demon covered its eyes in fear. The demon Marcus had just stabbed burst, and the small demon was covered in pasty cement-like liquid. The small demon grimaced in disgust. Marcus swung his sword around and down at the next demon that came running at him. He sliced it clean in half and it burst. Marcus felt a sharp pain in his stomach. He looked down and noticed a small dagger sticking out of his stomach on the right side. He flicked his sword and the small demon flew off and bounced off the wall before bursting, as Marcus turned to see the hooded figure. He readied his sword and was about to rush at the figure as it disappeared. He grabbed the third demon by the shoulder and stabbed it through the stomach. The last demon disappeared. Marcus grabbed Ben and flew up into the sky. Ben didn't even see Marcus open his wings. Marcus flew up to the bell tower of St. Andrews church and threw Ben down on the floor. Ben landed awkwardly and turned around to look at Marcus, who was standing in the open archway to the bell tower. He still hadn't seen his wings. "He must have closed them straight away," Ben thought.

Marcus reached down to the dagger sticking out of his stomach and pulled it out and dropped it on the floor. He stripped off his jacket and his hooded sweatshirt, and was wearing a tight blue t-shirt underneath. It was stained where the dagger was. Marcus grabbed the hole in his shirt and ripped it open to reveal a large wound that seemed to have a black substance staining his skin around it. The dagger looked like it went in pretty deep as Marcus was staggering, almost as if he was very drunk. He started walking backwards towards the open arch and Ben leapt up off the ground and grabbed him before he fell out. Marcus stood upright. "Ben, I..." he tried to speak. "Get help." He fell to the floor.

Ben fell to his knees at Marcus' side. "Marcus, no!" he said.

Marcus didn't respond. Ben pulled the rip in the t-shirt open a little more. It looked like blood was seeping out of the wound. Ben cupped his hands over the wound and closed his eyes. He concentrated as hard as he could and channeled all of his energy into his hands. A bright glow came from underneath his cupped hands over Marcus' stomach. Ben opened his eyes and stared in disbelief. He fought to keep concentration, and nearly passed out himself from the sheer power it consumed from him. The light died away. He took his hands away from the wound and blinked a few times to fight off the exhaustion. The wound had healed. He let out a gasp of triumph which was almost two breaths in one. He grabbed Marcus' jacket off the floor and threw it over him as he walked to the archway they came in from, and sat on the edge to regain his strength, whilst trying to figure out what had just happened.

* * *

Arus sat by a fire inside his cave. It was snowing outside, and the cave was very high up on a mountain. The wind howled through the opening and the fire flickered furiously. The white walls were illuminated yellow by the glow of the fire, and the few trinkets Arus had were scattered about. His sword, 'Beast', was up on the wall like a trophy. It was the sword he had made when he became the Commander of Battle, before Marcus. It was an impressive blade, only second in his opinion, to the Sword of the Angels. The metal he used to forge it was unlike anything he had seen before, and since the Commander of Battle is allowed to scour Heaven, Earth, Hell and Purgatory for the metal they used, he was rather convinced no one could find a similar piece. Although, he was annoyed at himself when Marcus found the metal to create his sword. "Why didn't I think of that?" Arus had thought.

Marcus had asked God for a piece of Heaven itself, and God was overjoyed to hand it over. It was probably one of the defining characteristics that made it so powerful. A weapon crafted from the very substance that Heaven is made up of, forged in the fires of Hell by the angel who may or may not become the most powerful they'd ever seen. Nonetheless, Arus was proud of Marcus. He sat there deep in thought, knowing his son had succeeded in retrieving the sword, knowing that this was still only the beginning. Arus was a battle worn soldier. He had fought in countless wars, and knew very well that there was always a calm before the storm. He just hoped Marcus knew it. He picked up his crossbow and aimed it carefully at the entrance to his cave as a feeling trickled in his senses. He sniffed the air slightly, and smelt an array of odours ranging from leather, to seduction, to death and decay; smells he was all too familiar with. He disarmed his crossbow and lay it down on the ground by the fire as he stood up and watched Eligos approach; her leathery outfit - or lack thereof - her wings out, and a somewhat deflated look on her face. He wasn't pleased to see her, although he took some comfort in knowing that Marcus hadn't killed her.

"Hello, lover," she called.

Arus grimaced at the thought. "I have never been, nor will I ever be, your lover."

"Now, now, that's no way to treat an old friend."

Arus sat down and started to stoke the fire. He kept Eligos in his peripheries, as he watched the flame flicker back and forth. "What do you want?" he asked.

Eligos continued to walk around the cave, taking in the details, noticing his sword on the wall. "Just a chat, darling. As you know, our agreement still stands."

"I know, my offspring are forbidden from killing you. You're not dead, are you? By the way, how's Orias?"

Eligos gave him a menacing look. "The stupid fool. More muscles than brains. Even I'm not stupid enough to take on your son alone."

Arus raised his eyebrows. "So you *are* afraid of him."

Eligos darted her eyes at Arus, but he kept his nonchalant exterior. "Good. You should be."

Eligos positioned herself on the opposite side of the fire to Arus. "Why should I fear something that can't kill me?"

Arus smirked. "Can't? Or won't?"

"He can't hurt me!" Her shout echoed through the cave.

Arus remained unimpressed. "Yes, he can. He doesn't have to kill you, to hurt you."

Eligos leapt over the fire flawlessly, landing directly onto Arus' lap, and staring straight into his eyes. A blue glow appeared in her mouth. "Keep your boy in check, or I'll be sure to fulfil my promise. Without my demise, if necessary."

Eligos felt something sharp ever so slightly digging into her stomach. She looked down to see a knife in Arus' hand, resting on the skin of her stomach. "And if I were to kill you? You said only my offspring, right?"

Eligos stood up. "You're going to pay for that threat, very dearly. Night night, precious."

Eligos disappeared.

* * *

Marcus opened his eyes and looked around him. He noticed the large bell in the middle of the room and the four archways, one on each of the four walls. He noticed Ben sitting in one of them. He sat up quickly and checked his wound. Ben turned around after hearing the noise. He stood up and walked over to Marcus sitting up on the floor. "What happened to the wound?" Marcus asked.

"I healed you," Ben said.

Marcus laughed. "Very funny. What really happened? Who came?"

"No one," Ben said, "I healed you myself."

Marcus knew when Ben was lying, and he knew that this time he wasn't lying. "That's impossible, Ben," Marcus said. "Only the Seraphim can heal other angels. You're just an angel. If it were you that was stabbed, I'd be able to heal you. Not the other way around."

Ben looked at Marcus. "I thought you were a Cherub."

Marcus' wings began to seep out of his back. The gold haze formed into sharp points and grew even larger. Ben looked up at the golden wings in awe. "Your wings," he said, "they've changed".

"After I went back to Heaven, I had a training session with Michael. He wanted to test me out now that I have my sword back. I actually beat him, and all of a sudden, this surge of power went through my body like lightning. When I looked up at my wings, they were gold. I am now Seraphim," Marcus said.

"My wings have changed a little too," Ben said. He let his wings seep out of his back. Marcus looked up to humour him about the colouration, when he noticed that they were slightly yellow, just a little off white.

"No, it's not possible," Marcus said.

"What's not possible?" Ben asked.

Marcus stood up and looked at Ben with bewilderment in his eyes. "It's you."

"What's me?"

Marcus sat sideways in the archway and Ben sat opposite him. "The Revelation speaks of a human becoming an angel. It says we will know who he is by his wings. Apparently they will go straight to gold. This human angel will become a Seraph straight away. I just can't believe it's you," Marcus said.

"But they're a little yellow, not gold," Ben said.

"There's no such thing. Angels are white, Archangels are brown, Powers are bronze, Principalities are light grey, Dominions are dark grey, Thrones are silver, Ophanim are purple, Cherubim are blue or red, and Seraphim are gold. There's no yellow. If your wings are yellow, it means you're on your way to becoming a Seraph. Now I know why they're after you."

"Why?" Ben asked.

"Because you're the human angel that the Revelation talks about."

"Why am I finding this a little difficult to believe? So I'm some sort of chosen one?"

"I don't like that cliché. But yes, in a sense," Marcus said.

"So who's after me?" Ben asked.

Marcus grabbed his jacket and pulled a packet of cigarettes out of the breast pocket. He pulled out a cigarette and put it in his mouth and grabbed his lighter out of his pants pocket. He lit the cigarette and breathed out the smoke with a deep breath. "Out of anything and anyone, who is the last being in existence you would want after you?" Marcus asked.

"The devil?" Ben asked.

"Other than him," Marcus said.

Ben thought for a long second, looking up and to the right as if he was trying to access certain data from that side of his brain. "I'd say you," Ben said.

Marcus took a long drag on his cigarette and looked Ben in the eyes. "That's pretty much who's after you."

Ben moved a little closer to the wall uncomfortably. "Not me, you idiot. His name is Lucas, and he's a demon. He was made from my blood. So technically, he is me."

"Lucas? An evil twin? And a chosen one. What was that word you used before? Cliché?" Ben laughed.

Marcus looked at him with narrow eyes. "Am I laughing?"

"You're not joking," Ben said in shock.

"No, I'm not."

"How did they get your blood?" Ben asked.

Marcus took another drag of his cigarette. "Percy. Years ago,"

"Oh shit!" Ben said, "And who created him?"

"A devil by the name of Dorian."

"So, that's who sent Lucas after me?" Ben asked.

"Can't be, Dorian is dead. I killed him myself, about forty years ago," Marcus said.

"Dead? You mean in Purgatory," Ben said.

"No, dead," Marcus said, "I killed him in Purgatory. He isn't coming back."

"So, who then?" Ben asked.

"I don't know, but I'm going to find out," Marcus said.

"What do we do now?" Ben asked.

"Let's go see Lucifer," Marcus replied.

CHAPTER II

Marcus and Ben were standing in the large room at the end of the hallway facing the door. They had transported from the bell tower at St. Andrews straight into Lucifer's white house amongst the fields of corpses. Lucifer was sprawled across his throne like chair with his legs hanging over the side. There were two angels standing either side of Lucifer with their blue wings floating above them. Ben and Marcus turned around towards Lucifer as he looked them up and down. "It's a bit soon to have missed me, isn't it?" Lucifer asked, "What's happened?"

Marcus walked over to another chair in the room and slumped himself down in it. "Someone has sent Lucas after Ben. He was attacked in the street tonight," Marcus said.

"Oh and you came to his rescue. My hero!" he joked, "Who could have sent him? Dorian is dead. Do you think he's acting on his own?"

"He wouldn't," Marcus said, "That's the one thing we don't have in common. There's always somebody pulling his strings."

Lucifer stroked his chin with his thumb and fore finger. He stood up and paced around the room a bit before looking at his chair. His thoughts raced a little longer. "Lucas was here," He said.

"When?" Marcus asked.

"When we were cleansing Hell, after you got your sword back. I completely forgot about it, as we were so hell bent - pardon the pun - on our task. He was sitting right there, in my seat."

Marcus stood up. "That means he's been watching us. Closely."

Lucifer nodded in agreement. He looked at Ben. "Why would somebody send Lucas after you?" he asked.

"Ben, show him," Marcus said.

Ben let his wings seep out of his back slowly. He looked as if he was almost ashamed of their colour. Not white, but off white; as if they were dirty. Lucifer stood up slowly and stared. "You?" he asked, "Are you serious?"

"They're yellow, aren't they?" Marcus asked.

"It's true. The Revelation is true!" Lucifer said as he descended down the three steps surrounding his throne. He grabbed Ben on the shoulders. "It's you! I can't believe this is actually happening."

"Believe it," Marcus said, "because now we have a problem on our hands."

"What problem?" Lucifer asked.

"If Lucas knows, then who else knows?" Marcus asked, staring at the floor.

"Good point. That is a problem. I'd love to know who put him up to it," Lucifer said.

"I'll find out." Marcus said, "In the meantime, Ben isn't safe on Earth, or here. We have to take him to Heaven."

"I agree, let's go," Lucifer said.

The three of them walked out of the room and down the large hallway, heading for the exit. As they stepped outside, they all opened their wings and took off in flight. Ben looked down at the fields of corpses and closed his eyes to stop himself from looking at the gruesome sight. They flew above the city where the devils roamed, but none of them came near as they made their way towards the exit high up on the mountain. They landed at the foot of the steps and began to ascend up to the rocky wall that led out to Earth. Ben looked back at Hell and walked up the steps in deep thought in between Marcus and Lucifer. They walked through the rock face and stepped out at the foot of Devils Tower as Ben turned around and put his hand through the wall. He looked at Marcus. "What?" Marcus asked.

"I understand why they can't escape through the gate, but what if they got up here? Couldn't they just walk back to Earth?" Ben asked.

"Humans can't pass through there. They'd just end up coming to a rock wall."

Ben turned his head to the side. "But I did..."

"No," Marcus said, "I pulled you through. Plus, you were already the descendant of an angel. Now let's go."

They flew up to the top and up the staircase to the battleground as they landed and walked towards the gates. Peter gave them a small nod as they approached, and Marcus flung the doors open. Ben looked down at the blue carpet-like street and remembered the first time he saw it, just days ago. His eyes looked down the carpet all the way to the end where the pearl staircase led up to God. Marcus and Lucifer began walking quickly towards it, and Ben followed reluctantly. They saw Michael at the foot of the stairs. He walked over to them with intrigue in his eyes. "What's going on?" he asked in his deep booming voice.

"Somebody has sent Lucas after Ben," Lucifer explained.

"What, why?" Michael asked.

"Are we gonna have to tell this story to everyone we see?" Ben asked.

"Look at his wings," Marcus said.

A crowd of angels was already forming around them to see Ben's' wings. They were all staring in awe. Michael looked at them and then back at Marcus. "The Revelation," he said.

Ben looked up to the staircase and noticed that God was already making his way down the stairs. He made his way over to Ben and began to circle him slowly. Ben felt like the Mona Lisa, on display with everybody in awe of it. Not only that, but God himself was circling him and inspecting him closely. It all felt so surreal to Ben. God looked at Marcus. "He is special. We can't let them get their hands on him," he said.

"That's why I brought him here," Marcus said, "Michael, I need you to train him, and fast. I want those wings as gold as yours when I get back."

"Where are you going?" Ben asked.

"To get some answers," Marcus said. Marcus disappeared.

"Alright then. Follow me, Ben," Michael said.

Michael began walking to the right of the stairs. Ben and Lucifer both followed him. He walked quickly and turned to walk into one of the beautiful pearl-like buildings. They walked into a large white room with weapons all over one of the walls. The floor was white, but soft; almost like it was padded. It was cushy under Ben's' feet. He looked down at it and bounced a little. Michael grabbed two swords off of the wall and handed one to Ben. "Let's see what you've got, kid," he said.

"He's pretty good," Lucifer said.

Ben looked over at Lucifer. Michael lunged forward at Ben with his sword. Ben quickly stood back and deflected the blow with his own sword. Michael started circling Ben and came at him from the side. Ben stepped back and blocked again. He threw his right shoulder backwards and spun around to come at Michael backhanded. Michael blocked quickly and stepped back to look Ben up and down. "You *are* pretty good," he said.

Ben walked over to the wall and put the sword back in its place. He walked along the wall looking at all the weapons, and stopped and pulled two bow staffs off the wall. He threw one to Michael who caught it one-handed, while the sword in his other hand disappeared. "Now, let's see what *you've* got," Ben said.

Ben twirled the staff in his fingers and raised it above his head, running at Michael with it spinning in his hand. He crouched just before he reached Michael, and swung at his feet. Michael jumped to avoid being hit and came at Ben with a two-handed strike from above, but Ben corrected and blocked it with the staff. Ben slid his hands apart so that one hand was on each end of the grip. He jabbed Michael in the stomach and spun the staff around, hitting him on the shoulder. He brought one end of the staff down to the ground and swept it under Michael's feet. Michael fell to the floor.

The yellow in Ben's wings became a bit brighter. Michael stood up and walked over to the wall. He put the bow staff back on the wall and took one of the swords off. It was a bastard sword, double edged, and heavy, with what looked like steel horns protruding from the hilt, above where the main hand would hold it. The handle was wrapped in a fine leather, and a jewel of some kind was set in snugly, right at the bottom. He walked over to Ben. "Here, I made this many years ago. I used it in battle many times. It is very dear to me. I want you to have it," he said.

"What for?" Ben asked.

"Because you deserve it," Michael said, "You will become a truly great warrior."

***

Marcus banged on the front door of the house that Samael was living in. The door opened an inch, and an eye peered out at Marcus. The eye disappeared and the door closed. "It's Marcus," the man said to Sam, "and he's alone."

Sam was sitting in one of the armchairs looking long ways across the coffee table. In the armchair at the other end was Lucas. Sam stared at Lucas. He was wearing a black suede jacket with jeans, and his hair was short and black. Other than that, he looked identical to Marcus. "Get out of here," Sam said.

Lucas got up out of the armchair and walked around it toward a door in the back of the room. He walked through the door, into a dimly lit kitchen. There was a door at the back of the kitchen that led out into the back yard. He stepped over to it and opened it towards him and stepped outside. He closed the door quietly behind him as he reached into his jacket breast pocket and pulled out a cigarette. Lucas pulled a lighter out of his jeans pocket and lit the cigarette as he leaned against the wall next to the door. Inside, Sam nodded to the man by the door who turned around, unlinked the chain and opened the door. Marcus walked in slowly. He stopped just inside the doorway and looked around the room. He saw the same faces from his last visit, with a few additions. There were two men sitting on the large couch against the wall, Sam was sitting in the armchair to the right, and the armchair on the left was empty. There were two other men leaning against the wall on Marcus' right. They looked at him quizzically. Marcus noticed a baseball bat leaning against the wall in between them as he walked to the empty armchair and sat down. He looked across at Sam with questions in his eyes. "Welcome back," Sam said.

"I find it odd that there are three men standing in the room and one empty chair. So either you have another guest, or fatso has given up his seat for me."

"What do you want?" Sam asked.

"Why do you assume I want something?" Marcus asked.

"Why else do you come here?"

"Good point. In all the times I've come here, the door has been opened in seconds, and you have been a little more hospitable. What's going on?" Marcus asked.

"Maybe I'm busy."

"You've always got time for me Sam, remember that. Tell me about Lucas," he said.

One of the men leaning against the wall picked up the baseball bat. Marcus noticed it instantly. "New recruits?" he asked.

"Fresh from the ground," Sam replied.

"Guess they don't know who I am then," Marcus said.

"Nope," Sam replied, "but I'm sure you'll show them soon enough."

The man with the bat started to walk over to where Marcus was sitting. He circled around the chair so that he was standing behind Marcus. "Would you like a drink?" Sam asked.

"I'd love one, thanks. The usual," Marcus replied.

Sam got up out of his chair and walked around the chair Marcus was sitting in, and past the man with the bat. He gave him a stern look and shook his head as a deterrence. It was a look that said *don't go there*. He proceeded to walk out through the door at the back of the room and into the kitchen. He looked around nervously, making sure Lucas was gone, and started to make a drink for Marcus. In the lounge room, Marcus turned to look at the man with the bat. He had a bald head and a goatee surrounding his mouth like a large black circle. Marcus looked at the bat in his hand. He was holding it ready with a clenched fist wrapped around the handle. It was a wooden bat with some sort of label running down it near the end. Marcus liked baseball bats. They were like blunt swords. Sam came back into the room with a glass in each hand. Both glasses had a reddish black liquid in them. He sat one down in front of Marcus and took a sip out of the other one as he sat back down. Marcus picked up the drink and took a sip. "Don't worry," Sam said, "It's only red label, so the coke didn't ruin it."

"Good man. So tell me about Lucas," he said again.

The man standing behind Marcus raised the bat to his shoulder. Marcus pointed straight at him. "If you hit me with that, I will take you to somewhere even your worst nightmares would fear. I just might leave you there too," he warned, putting his hand down.

The bat came swinging down at the side of his head, and hit Marcus right on the temple. He barely flinched, and his head tilted sideways with the momentum. He stood up and shrugged his jacket into place. "You shouldn't have done that," Sam said.

Marcus turned around and walked towards the man with the bat. The man looked uneasy, wondering how Marcus hadn't been hurt. He started walking backwards just as Marcus reached under his jacket and pulled out his sword. The man dropped the bat instantly and backed up a lot quicker. Marcus grabbed him around the throat and opened his gold wings. They began floating and the ground sunk beneath them. The man struggled to look down and saw decaying bodies ripping the flesh off of other decaying bodies. The ground beneath them was like mud, or wet cement. All of the animated corpses were covered in this mud-like liquid. They all looked up at Marcus with this man, and began climbing on top of each other to reach up to them. Marcus floated down a little lower. A decayed hand wrapped itself around the man's leg as Marcus lowered him, and he let out a horrified scream. Marcus dropped him and he fell to Sam's lounge room floor. He looked at his ankle and grabbed at it anxiously, as if something was still attached to it, and then around at the room in shock. He stood up and looked at Marcus with fear in his eyes.

"Did you enjoy that? Hit me with the baseball bat again. I'll leave you there," Marcus said. He put his sword back up underneath his jacket and sat back down in the armchair.

"Was that the sword?" Sam asked.

"The one and only," Marcus replied.

"Wow, can I see it?"

"No, tell me about Lucas!" Marcus shouted.

Sam took another sip of his drink. "I don't know what to tell you, he's a demon that was created from your blood," he said.

"I know that, you idiot. Tell me what he's up to," Marcus said.

"Why would I know what he's up to?" Sam asked.

"Because he's your friend," Marcus said.

"Well I haven't seen him, so I wouldn't know," Sam replied.

***

Ben was standing in the room with the padded floor. He was up against the wall and Lucifer and Michael were at the other end of the room against the other wall. The wall with the weapons was to his right. He was breathing heavily and trying to concentrate. "Okay Ben, the way to do this is to want to be over here more than anything. That's how you have to think. Close your eyes, and when I count to three, transport yourself over here. Are you ready?" Lucifer asked.

"I guess so," Ben said. He closed his eyes and took a deep breath. Michael and Lucifer watched him anxiously.

"Okay. One, two, three," Lucifer counted.

Ben disappeared. Lucifer and Michael looked all around the room, but he wasn't anywhere to be seen. They looked at each other. "If he didn't come over here," Lucifer asked, "Where did he go?"

***

Lucas flicked his cigarette onto the concrete and squashed it with his boot. He walked over to the back fence and put one hand over the top of it, looking back towards the house and around the yard to make sure the coast was clear. He put his other hand on top of the fence and peered over. The alley way behind the house was empty. He lifted himself up and threw his whole body over the fence in one quick movement. He landed facing the fence, and then turned to walk away and came face to face with Ben. He looked him up and down as anger filled his eyes. "Marcus?" Ben asked, "What did you do to your hair?"

Lucas touched the top of his head and looked at Ben. A sly smile fell over his face. "I cut it, what do you think?" Lucas asked.

"I think you're copying me a little too much," Ben laughed. Lucas smiled a little more.

***

"You lying to me?" Marcus asked.

"You know I wouldn't, Marcus," Sam replied.

Marcus stood up. He stepped around the coffee table and leaned over Sam's chair, with distrust in his eyes. He glared at Sam as his senses picked up on a bad vibe. Something wasn't right. He stood up and let his mind clear as he listened very carefully to all the sounds around him. He smelt the air and closed his eyes to hone in on what it was he had sensed. It was difficult for him to pin down the scents that filled his nose, but mostly because the smell of his own blood was clouding his judgement. His own blood was nearby. And so was Ben's. "He's here," Marcus said.

"Who?" Sam asked.

Marcus turned and ran through the kitchen and out the back door. He sprinted toward the back fence and sprung off his feet, shooting up like a basketball player, landing with his feet balanced perfectly on the top of the fence as his golden wings shot out of his back. He saw Ben, standing face to face with Lucas. Ben stared up at Marcus in awe, unsure of what was going on, but noticed the wings. In front of him he saw two of Marcus, one with long brown hair and golden wings, one with short black hair, and seemingly, no wings. A sudden realisation hit him. He remembered Marcus talking about Lucas being made from his blood. Fear suddenly fell over his face as his stomach knotted up. Lucas turned to see what had caught Ben's attention and locked eyes with Marcus. They stared at each other for a moment as Ben took the opportunity to take off in flight. Normally he wouldn't run from a fight, but he'd rather not take on a demon that was created with Marcus' blood. He opened his wings and flew away as fast as he could. Marcus lunged himself off of the fence and tackled Lucas. The momentum caused them both to go tumbling toward the grass on the other side of the alley. There was a barbed wire fence separating the lane from the grass, and Marcus and Lucas were headed straight for it, fumbling and rolling. Marcus noticed it in just enough time as he held out his hand and his sword appeared just before they hit the fence. The sword cut through the barbed wire like butter, as it twanged and recoiled against itself, parting for the two of them to roll through. They stopped rolling on the grass with Marcus on top. He raised his sword to strike as Lucas kicked him off and quickly jumped to his feet. They were standing facing each other, as Marcus let his sword disappear. Lucas knew better than to take his eyes off Marcus, although he wanted to see where Ben had gone. He kept his stare.

Ben had perched himself on a rooftop in the distance, keeping an eye on what was going on between Marcus and Lucas. His mind began to wander. This new world he had gotten himself caught up in scared the shit out of him, yet he always embraced a challenge. He was now training with not only the elite, but with the super-fucking-natural elite. He should relish the opportunity to take on such a demon. He watched closely, waiting to see what would unfold before him, and waiting to see whether he should get involved.

Lucas moved his head to the left, trying to use his peripheries to see behind him. His eyes moved too far, and Marcus lunged forward and right into his blind spot. His knee came up as he darted straight for Lucas' stomach, and collided with a mighty force. Lucas keeled over in pain and shock, but had to react quickly. His head was already down beside Marcus' hip, possibly the worst place it could be. He fought to regain his composure and was in the process of readying himself when the inevitable happened. Marcus had wrapped his arm around Lucas' neck in a reverse headlock. What was worse, Marcus had already locked his right hand behind Lucas' shoulder from underneath his neck, whilst pushing Lucas' right wrist against his thigh, straightening his arm against the elbow. Putting enough pressure on the arm from this position would break it, and Lucas knew this. If he squirmed, it would only tighten Marcus' grip. Marcus put his left hand on Lucas' elbow, putting the slightest amount of pressure, bringing it almost to breaking point.

Lucas brought his left arm up to Marcus' arm around his neck and grabbed and twisted it. Marcus lost his grip and Lucas had his arm freed slightly. His wings erupted from his back. They were black and leathery, almost like bats wings, and since Marcus' hands were occupied, he wouldn't expect it. Lucas' wings flapped and hit Marcus on either side of the head, causing Marcus to lose his balance and stumble backwards. Lucas turned to the direction Ben had flown off in and saw him perched on the rooftop. Ben panicked and quickly leapt off the roof in flight as Lucas readied himself to pursue. He was stopped instantly. Marcus had grabbed Lucas by the wings, right near his shoulder blades. He turned around and flipped Lucas over the top of him by the wings, as Lucas landed on the ground in front of Marcus. He stood up and tried to take off after Ben again. He got clear of Marcus, but Marcus leapt up and grabbed hold of his ankles. Marcus hung in the air for a second, using all the strength he could to drag Lucas back down. He yanked on Lucas' ankles and threw him down to the ground. He reached under his jacket and pulled out his sword. Lucas stood up and disappeared. Marcus looked all around him. "Shit," he said.

He took off in the air after Ben, who was flying so fast that Marcus found it difficult to keep up. Marcus eventually caught him and grabbed onto him. Ben gasped in shock and began to panic. "It's me! It's me!" Marcus shouted.

Marcus instantly transported them and they both fell onto the padded floor in the training room. They looked up and saw Lucifer and Michael staring in disbelief. "Well, that was unexpected," Lucifer said, "At least now we know he can transport."

Marcus stood up and stared at Lucifer with anger in his eyes. "Yeah, you obviously taught him really well. What did you tell him to do?" Marcus asked.

"He stood at one end of the room and us at the other, and Lucifer told him that he wanted to be on our side of the room more than anything," Michael said.

"It's easier than that. I've taught him his whole adult life. He's a quick learner, he just has to believe in himself. Thanks to you guys, he just met Lucas. Lucky I was there," Marcus said. Marcus walked over to Lucifer and Michael and turned to face Ben. "Ben, go stand at that wall and close your eyes," he said as he pointed at the far wall. Ben walked towards the wall and turned around to face them. The wall of weapons was on his right again. He closed his eyes. "Now when you open your eyes, you will be standing over here, right next to me. I want you to count to three in your head and imagine it, just like with the flying. Put the image in your head, and believe it, then open your eyes," Marcus said.

Ben took a deep breath and counted to three in his head. He closed his eyes and pictured himself doing it, trying to believe it would happen just by willing it to. He opened his eyes and looked at the far wall. Marcus, Lucifer and Michael weren't there. The wall of weapons was now on his left. He looked to his left and saw Marcus standing right next to him. He opened his eyes wide in awe. "I did it!" he shouted.

"You see?" Marcus said, "All you have to do is believe it, and it'll happen."

"So where did he go before?" Lucifer asked.

"To where I was, at Sam's place. He bumped into Lucas, and I sensed them. I got there just in time," Marcus said.

"Did you kill him?" Lucifer asked.

"No, I didn't get the chance."

"So what do we do now?" Ben asked.
"I have some demons to exterminate. Michael? Wings gold when I get back, okay?" Marcus said.

"Okay okay, you get your sword and all of a sudden you're the man in charge," Michael said.

Marcus gave a confident, yet surly look. "Commander of Battle?" he asked.

Michael nodded. "Yes yes, I know. Wings gold."

Marcus walked out the door and back onto the blue carpeted street, looking for someone in particular. Ben looked at Michael who didn't look mad or intimidated. He was watching Marcus with a sense of pride. It was like a father watching a child accomplish the impossible. Michael nodded to himself in satisfaction. "He's all grown up now," he said.

Ben looked down at the floor in slight disappointment. He always wanted to be a father. The thought of bringing up a child and teaching them all about the world, how to walk, talk, ride a bike, being able to play with them, and answer every question that was ever asked. Why is the sky blue? Why is grass green? Why do you have a moustache? Why do you have jeans on? And watching them turn into a man or a woman. Guiding them through ups and downs that life throws at you. Now all he could think of was how he would ever become a father as an angel? The only time he came close was with his ex-girlfriend, Alexandra. Everyone called her Alex, and Ben loved her dearly. Things didn't work out and Ben moved away to the city. He always wished that he could someday go back and fix things, and start a family. But now, he was basically immortal. No longer human. No longer able to go back. Regret began to fill his mind. He was deep in thought as Lucifer stared at him, noticing the doubt and pain in his eyes. He knew something was up. "Let's take a break," Lucifer said.

Ben came out of his stupor and looked at Lucifer, and realised that Lucifer had noticed his demeanour. Ben suddenly corrected his stance and posture, standing upright as he let his mind slow and come back to reality, just like Marcus had taught him. He stretched his elbows behind him and tilted his head from side to side to stretch it. "Nah, let's do this. I'm good."

Lucifer put his hand on Ben's shoulder and look into his eyes. "No," he said, "you're not."

Ben noticed the calming effect Lucifer's hypnotic eyes had on him; like a cool breeze extruded from them and enhanced his relaxation. He needed to talk to someone. He needed to vent. He had bottled up so much after becoming an angel with everything that had happened, he hadn't had the chance to open up and express his true feelings about his situation. He felt like a secondary character in his own story, like a bit player, who was going to be the first to fall in battle. The thirty-second man, that you send in to buy you time in a fight. Cannon fodder. His eyes began to water as he looked at Lucifer again, who hadn't shifted his gaze. Ben lunged forward and threw his arms around Lucifer in a large hug. Stunned, Lucifer hugged him back, understanding completely. He had spent so much time with humans, and always heard that there were things they wish they could have done. He didn't understand in the sense of experience, as he had never experienced any human emotion. He was always bitter, but never sad. Sadness, was something he didn't understand. The situation, he knew all too well. He felt for Ben. He was really beginning to like the kid. The embrace had sealed their friendship. They were no longer acquaintances; they were now brothers. Ben stepped back from the hug and looked up at Lucifer. "Let's talk, you and I," Lucifer said.

***

Marcus found two cherubs sitting in a clearing on the other side of the steps that led up to God. They were in conversation amongst themselves, and they stood as Marcus approached. He knew them well; they were warriors in his army, and had fought many battles. Both were not much bigger than Marcus himself. One had brown hair, and one had black hair. "Sarandiel, Ophaniel, I need to talk to you."

"What's the problem?" Sarandiel asked, "Still have a beef with Samael?"

Ophaniel cracked a slight grin. "You know where he is?"

Marcus nodded. "I'm headed there right now. He's just lied to me for the last time." Marcus grabbed them both by a shoulder each and transported them away.

***

Lucifer and Ben walked away from the room with the padded floor and in the opposite direction of the steps. They found themselves in a large clearing, with a wonderful landscape in front of them. Ben had never seen this part of Heaven before and looked in awe. It looked like it went on for miles and miles. It was like a bustling city and countryside, with beaches, rivers, hills, and buildings. Skyscrapers so tall it almost hurt his neck to look at the top. Millions of people. All happy, all enjoying themselves. It looked like a Utopia. Ben realised instantly. This was Heaven. He had seen Hell; the torment, the pain; this was the opposite. He smiled. "I thought you might like to see this," Lucifer said.

Ben continued to look around. Everyone was doing something different. Such an assortment of different tasks. People happy together, people happy alone, doing what it looked like they loved. "How does it work?" Ben asked.

"You get to choose. Every day, you can open your life like a book; pick a day, relive it. Or you can do something you never got the chance to try. The choice is yours.

Ben nodded, "Now that's Heaven".

There was a river nearby. Ben could hear it rushing and heard all the familiar sounds he had heard on earth. Birds chirping, and all sorts of nature flooded his senses as they walked towards it. They found a quiet spot on the rocks near the river, with only the sounds of nature surrounding them. Lucifer started the conversation, "Talk to me. What's in your head? I saw that look in your eyes. You doubt something, regret something. You're unsure".

Ben looked down. "I never got to become a father."

Lucifer gave him a surprised look. He thought for a second and let Ben sit with what he had said. "That's it?"

Ben looked at Lucifer. "What do you mean, that's it?"

"Well, you're not dead, you know. There's still a way."

Ben looked confused. He didn't quite understand. He knew that Lucifer and Marcus were brothers, and that Arus was their father. Could he become a father as an angel? Arus had a child with a human, although it was heavily frowned upon. There could still be a chance. The only problem was, his heart still yearned for Alexandra. He hadn't properly met any female angels; he wasn't even sure how to go about having a relationship with one. Everything was all still so new. He had a task. He had to train. He had to get his wings to gold. He had to become the Human Angel. His mind slowed as everything fell into perspective. He had stick to his conviction. He chose this path, and he never quit anything. He wanted to see it through. That was the priority. He looked at Lucifer. "You know what? You're right. I have plenty of time. The Revelation, however, is on our doorstep. That is the priority."

Lucifer nodded. "You're tougher than you look, kid. I've seen this conundrum break the cruelest of men."

Ben looked dumbfounded. "I'm amazed at the people you must have met. I say that, yet here I am, in Heaven, talking to Lucifer. I guess I should consider myself lucky."

Lucifer laughed, "You're in Heaven, talking to me, kid. I wouldn't consider yourself that lucky. Most people ask about God".

Ben laughed as well. "Yeah, well I am in a pretty strange situation. With you being in Heaven, and all. You're a lot better company than you give yourself credit for. You saw I was struggling with something, you pulled me aside, and made me regain focus. I really appreciate that. You're a good man. Well, angel, devil, whatever the hell you are. You're a good friend. So thank you."

Lucifer sat up in reverence. It had been a long time since he had been called good. He half smiled. "No, thank you," he said quietly.

***

The door burst open and Marcus walked in with his sword in his hand. The man to the left of the door jumped at him, and he turned and ran his sword through the man's stomach. The man gasped in pain and burst into liquid. The man that was leaning against the wall ran at Marcus. Marcus head butted him and swung his sword around backhand, which sliced the man in two. The man burst as Marcus walked towards the back wall. He reached under his jacket and pulled out his dagger and flipped it so that the blade was in his hand. He threw it at one of the men sitting on the couch against the wall and it went straight through his forehead. Marcus leapt over the coffee table and pulled it out of the man's head before he exploded. He thrust the dagger into the chest of the other man sitting on the couch. Sam stood up and tried to run around the coffee table into the kitchen. Marcus jumped up and chased him through the door. He grabbed Sam around the throat from behind and turned to slam him against the wall. Marcus lifted Sam up against the wall by his throat. "You lied to me," Marcus said.

"I told you I don't know anything," Sam said as he squirmed.

"Yes, but you *do* know something. Do you want to lie to me again? I know he was here!"

Marcus held his sword up to Sam's throat. "Here, you wanted to see it, didn't you?"

"Okay!" he shouted, "I'll tell you."

"Who sent Lucas after Ben?" Marcus asked.
He dropped Sam onto the floor and turned around to face the back door. Sam rubbed his throat and sat up against the wall. "It's Dorian," he said.

Marcus turned around and stared at him. "That's impossible. Dorian is dead."

"Dorian *was* dead," Sam said.

"That can't be true. You know better than I do that if you die in Purgatory, you don't come back," Marcus said.

"I know, and believe me, a lot of us saw you do it. He's just back, I don't know how, but he is. It's him!" Sam shouted.

Marcus kicked him in the face. "Are you lying to me? Because if you are, I will send you back there so fast. Don't even get me started on who's waiting there for you."

"It's Dorian, I promise. They're in the big house on the hill, just east of here. McCully Avenue. Please don't send me back. I will never go back there," Sam pleaded.

"Sam, you're just full of lies today," Marcus said.

At that moment, Sarandiel and Ophaniel walked through the door with their blue wings above them. They stood on either side of Marcus and stared at Sam. "You *are* going back."

Marcus walked towards the door into the lounge room. "But I told you the truth!" Sam shouted.

"I'm not taking that chance," Marcus said.

Marcus closed the door and pulled a cigarette out of his jacket pocket. He pulled a chrome lighter out of his jeans pocket and lit the cigarette. He let the lighter burn for a few seconds and then threw it onto the couch in the puddle left from Sam's friends, and the couch burst into flames. He walked out the door, listening to Sam's screams coming from the kitchen as he took a long drag of his cigarette.

Marcus transported to his apartment and walked over to his bookshelf. He pushed on it and it rotated in the wall, revealing his second bookcase with all of his journals. He found 'E' and took out a book with 'Ethiopia' written on the spine, and opened it up to the inside of the back cover. There was a large ornate key attached to it with leather string. He removed the key and slid it into his pocket as he closed the book and returned it to the bookshelf. With that, he was instantly standing in Ethiopia, behind the chapel of the tablet. There was no one around, and against the wall was a large stone. It was about the same size as a chest, and rectangular, with a hole in the front, which looked like it was about the right size for the key Marcus took from his apartment. He took the key from his pocket and put it into the hole in the rock and turned it, as the ground started to vibrate. The stone separated in half, and parted in the middle as Marcus removed the key and put it back in his pocket. Underneath the stone was a staircase that led underneath the chapel. He walked down the staircase as the stone moved back into place above his head, as he descended into a small stone room that seemed as though it was carved by hand, into the very stone foundations the chapel was sitting on top of. There was an engraving on the wall above eye height, that was in a rather peculiar language.

It wasn't English, and it certainly wasn't angelic, nor demonic. It was Enochian; a language derived from humans many years previously, that they thought was the language of the angels. They were wrong. Marcus figured that even if anyone were able to stumble across it, they would never be able to figure out why it said what it said. There were other carvings in the wall - five different carvings - all symbolising something different. Anyone with any knowledge of powerful beings would understand what they meant. Marcus muttered a phrase in English, "The Rescinder Blade".

The ground began to shake again, as the wall in front of him began to part. The writing on the wall didn't say 'The Rescinder Blade', it said something else. He stepped through the gap in the wall and into his hidden library. There were bookshelves full of books, and more of his own journals. There was a shelf that held almost all the same titles as the one in his apartment, only there was one difference. Marcus stared at the journal between 'C' and 'E', with the word 'Downfall' carved into its leathery spine. He became almost catatonic, just staring at it, as if doing so would make it disappear, and thus somehow remove the event from his past. He shrugged off his discomfort and walked further into his library. There were weapons, upon weapons, upon weapons. His sword, the Sword of the Angels, was on the wall, in a space he had saved for it once he had retrieved it. His library was his safe house. His weapon when he allowed it to disappear, went to his library. There was also a stash of weapons hidden in his apartment, in case of emergency, but many of them came here. There were two pistols sitting on a stand on a bookshelf, both black, with silver trim. They were Marcus' Colt Dragoons. They were strapped in holsters by his side for many years. They too, gave him grim memories. One had a silver cross on the handle, and the other had a silver pentagram, upside down, with a rams head in it, because one could kill demons, and one could kill angels.

Marcus picked up the gun with the cross on it. It was the gun he'd used to kill Dorian all those years ago. Marcus had watched him go up in flames in Purgatory. The thought couldn't escape his mind. *How could he have survived?* he thought. Marcus put the gun back on the stand and turned to one of his bookshelves and began to look through it. There were all kinds of books there; some new, some old, and some very old. He pulled out a very old, large book and began sifting through the pages, flicking backwards and forwards, trying to find something, *anything* that could explain how Dorian was alive. He returned the book to the shelf and searched again, finding another very old, red covered leather bound book and pulled it out.

Flicking through the pages again, frustrated with determination to solve the mystery, he finally found the page he was looking for. He placed the book down on a desk with the page open and switched on an old lamp as he read the page. It was the Book of Purgatory, and the pages were made of skin, obviously skin from the occupants of Purgatory, bound in a cover that resembled the skin of demons. The page was titled 'Death', and was mostly about the cement-like liquid that plagued all of Purgatory. The book called it 'Ichor', and explained in great detail that it was an excretion from the bodies that roamed the place. Almost like blood, sweat, tears and shit all mixed in together with a great big dose of bone, sinew, guts and entrails. It was basically a liquefied form of the body. The book explained that when one is killed and sent to Purgatory, their bodies beforehand fill up with ichor, as they take its place within the realm. It fills up so fast that their bodies just implode into a mess on the floor. He continued reading as he got to what he was searching for and turned the page. It explained that when one is killed in Purgatory, their bodies are no longer bound and therefore, no longer needed. They turn to flames and ash, and disintegrate. It then went on to explain that if one outside of Purgatory wanted to do away with an enemy for good, and provided they were powerful enough, they could open a portal to Purgatory and smite their enemy, causing them to turn to flames and ash, and disintegrate. Marcus recalled that he had done exactly that to Baal in Ben's lounge room when Declan was killed, without even knowing it. He grinned slightly. "If one were powerful enough, hey?" he said as he continued reading.

The book finished by saying that there is no known form of life after Purgatory, since none have ever come back. "Bullshit!" Marcus shrieked.

He turned the next few pages to see if there were anything added after the fact, but nothing leapt out at him. He heard footsteps behind him and turned to see Arus walking towards him. He let out a sigh of relief. "Don't sneak up on me like that," he said.

"Hey, I made myself as obvious as possible. If I didn't, you would have pulled those guns thinking someone was actually sneaking up on you."

Marcus nodded. Arus was right, if he had heard someone sneaking, he would have been on guard straight away. He looked up at Arus with question in his eyes. Arus explained, "I opened the book in your apartment. The one that usually has the key in it. Noticed the key was missing, figured you'd be here. How's the kid doing?"

"The kid? Ben?"

"Yes, the one who is supposedly the Human Angel? Didn't think to tell me about that?"

Marcus sighed, "I was getting around to it, I've been busy". Marcus closed the book and returned it to the shelf.

"The Book of Purgatory? What's got you so interested in that?"

"Apparently, Dorian is alive," Marcus said, "and since I killed him in Purgatory years ago, I wondered if there is a way back. There doesn't appear to be, although I did find out that the sludge-like substance when you kill them, is called ichor. And after finding out what it actually is, I feel all the more disgusted having touched it."

"Well look at that, you didn't know everything," Arus remarked, "and I still prefer ichor to ectoplasm."

Marcus shuddered uncomfortably. "Yes, well we both know what usually follows ectoplasm."

They both stood in silence for a moment as Marcus stared at the floor. The thought of ectoplasm itself made them both extremely uncomfortable. It was something they had both experienced firsthand. The very essence of beings, plagued by the substance in the abyss. Not many knew of the abyss, for it was a place of absolute terror. The beings that lurked there were the things of nightmares. The abyss was part of the ethereal realm. Earth and all its occupants were known as the corporeal realm, which is where humanity resides. The ethereal realm was unseen to the naked eye from the corporeal realm. It contained beings known as Apparitions.

They had many categories. The first and second categories were your basic ghosts and ghouls; very common in the corporeal realm as they could very easily cross over. However, beneath the water, lay the abyss where the third and fourth categories lived. It was much harder for them to cross over, as it generally required an event on a cosmological scale. Any beings on earth from the abyss were very rare, and also extremely dangerous. It was once written that fools rush in, where angels fear to tread. That very sentiment itself was written of the abyss, as even angels fear those that dwell there; those who knew of it. Arus could see that something unconnected to the abyss was on Marcus' mind. Something was troubling him. "You're not just trying to figure out how

Dorian came back to make sure he doesn't do it again, are you? You're worried. You're trying to see if there is a way back for yourself, aren't you?"

Marcus sighed, "The angel will fall, and rise again with the great power that he was destined to behold".

Arus sat down. "What makes you think that means you? Lots of angels up there."

"The following sentence says the most powerful sword must belong to the most powerful angel. How could it not be me?"

Arus sighed, "He always was a cryptic bastard, wasn't he?"

Marcus sat forward and put his face into his hands, rubbing under his tired eyes with his fingers which then moved around to his temples. "Cryptic or not, couldn't he just tell me? Am I supposed to be playing this as if I'm going to die? Should I be making arrangements? Or setting up a contingency? Or a successor of sorts?"

"Don't act on that assumption. You have a task at hand. Just focus on that for now, and if the time comes, worry about it then."

Marcus nodded. "You're right. I guess I'd better get up there and take care of this."

"By the way," Arus started, "I received a visit from Eligos. She's got her eye fixed on you. Be very careful."

"Why am I not surprised? She's up to something."

"Something indeed," Arus said, "Be very careful, son. If you become the Archfiend..."

Marcus cut him off, "If I become the Archfiend, I expect you to end me".

Arus stood silently. The thought alone troubled him. "You can't ask that of me."

Marcus summoned a small chrome blade that looked very old, with two red stripes running up its handle. It was as if the blade and handle were all fashioned from one piece of metal. It was a powerful blade, and they both knew it well. The chrome handle glowed a furious red. Marcus held it flat against Arus' chest, giving it to him. "The Rescinder Blade."

Arus said, "I won't have anything to do with that. You should have destroyed this".

Marcus kept the blade flat against Arus' chest as his eyes filled with stubbornness. "It's the most powerful weapon we have."

"And the only weapon that could possibly kill God!" Arus shouted.

They stayed quiet for a moment, then Arus broke the silence, "If this were to fall into the wrong hands...."

"Which is why I'm giving it to you. Your weapons cache is a lot safer than mine."

Arus sighed as Marcus pushed the blade harder against his chest. "Promise me," Marcus said, "you will end me."
Arus slowly nodded and took the handle of the blade as he let it disappear and store itself among his own stash of weapons. "I promise," he said.

* * *

Marcus appeared in the training room next to the wall of weapons. Ben had his wings out and they were a green-gold colour. He looked at Marcus. "Hey, Marcus," he called. He walked over to Marcus and looked him up and down. He had a few patches of grey mud on his jeans. "What happened?" he asked.

"Just had a chat to some friends. Lucifer, can I talk to you for a second?" Marcus asked. He began to walk out the door and Lucifer followed him. They walked over to the steps below, where God was sitting. Ben and Michael came outside the room and stood out the front. "It's Dorian," Marcus said. Marcus was rubbing the palm of his left hand with the thumb on his right hand. He was looking down at the blue floor.

"Are you sure?" Lucifer asked, "But how?"

"I don't know. Sam said it's not far from his place in Staten Island. Well, his old place now. It's the big house on top of the hill. McCully Avenue"

Lucifer tilted his head to the side. "You killed Sam?"

"Not me, a few friends that have wanted to find him for a long time. What can I say? He lied to me. Now I have one request to ask you," Marcus said.

"What's that?"

Marcus looked up at Lucifer. "If something happens, don't bring Ben. At least not until he's almost ready."

Marcus disappeared, leaving Lucifer stunned as to what he meant. Ben had noticed that Marcus had gone and finished talking to Michael. "Excuse me," he said to Michael. He walked up to Lucifer and looked at him. "What did he say?"

"He didn't say much, but I think he's going to do something incredibly stupid," Lucifer replied.

"Like what?"

"I'm sure we'll find out very soon."

CHAPTER III

Marcus transported back to the entrance of his library and pulled his key out to open the lock in the stone as a faint scent hit his nose. He smelt leather, mixed with ichor and a very unwelcome scent that could be mistaken for women's perfume. It was unwelcome because Marcus knew the source. He put the key back into his pocket and turned around to see Eligos slowly walking toward him. She was dressed a lot less provocative, in a modern style outfit with leather pants and a black singlet top, with knee high boots. A slightly smug look fell across her face as she walked on with confidence. Marcus stood his ground and waited patiently as she came closer. Her face changed to serious as she came to a stop ten feet away from him. Marcus wasn't afraid, but he was alone. Any confrontation could very easily lead to her death, and ultimately his own fate would soon follow; whether that be his death, or his undoing. He decided it was best to proceed with caution, as he relaxed his clenched state of readiness, to appear non-threatening. Eligos noticed and took a deep breath as she too, relaxed. They both stared at each other for a long moment of silence until Eligos spoke. "I'm here to propose an agreement," she said.

Marcus raised an eyebrow and slowly stepped backward. He leaned against the wall next to the stone and pulled out a cigarette and lit it. He took a large puff and blew out the smoke in a small sigh, again, trying to look nonchalant. "To my knowledge," he started, "agreements with you don't work out so well for the other parties involved."

Eligos slowly walked closer as Marcus glanced at a spot on the ground in front of her. He watched her feet very closely as she slowed and stopped mid-stride just before the spot he was looking at. She looked down at the ground and took a small cautious step back and looked back at Marcus. A smirk lifted the corner of his mouth as he returned her gaze. "Consecrated ground," Marcus said, "I was kind of hoping you wouldn't notice."

Eligos almost smiled, but fought against it. Had she not noticed, she could have been very badly hurt, or worse, killed. A sinister thought crossed her mind which gave her a wicked smile. "I'm curious, was it you that consecrated it?"

Marcus stayed silent. It was him that had blessed the ground the chapel stood on, and the library beneath it had a very powerful consecration within the walls; one he came up with himself. It made his library and the chapel impenetrable. If anything evil were to cross that imaginary line surrounding it, they'd be done for. Marcus came to a sudden realisation. He knew why Eligos was asking. The situation had just become very dangerous. "From your silence, I'm going to say yes," Eligos said.

Marcus opened his mouth to speak, but couldn't come out with any words.

"So if I were to take one step this way…" She lifted her back foot to step forward as Marcus stepped forward from his lean against the wall. He stretched his arms in front of him in an attempt to stop her, but halfway through, realised she was bluffing. He had just given her the answer. "If I set one foot on this soil, my dear boy, I'd be dead. Since your pretty little hands are responsible for blessing the ground, I'd say that would mean you were responsible for my fate. Wouldn't you agree?"

"What do you want?" Marcus asked.

Eligos shifted her weight to her back foot and brought her front foot back to stand front on. Her eyes looked Marcus up and down with a hint of approval for what she saw. She liked him, but mostly because he resembled his father. Her mind wandered around the things she would like to do to him, both sexually and violently, maybe even both at the same time. Her mind came back to her task at hand. "I want the boy," she said.

Marcus narrowed his eyes and began to walk forward with confidence. She wanted Ben. The very thought stirred a fire within Marcus that he couldn't douse. It burned hotter than the very fires of Hell, like a white flash of fury that couldn't be extinguished. He stepped closer, eight feet away, seven feet, six feet. His rage grew as he stepped closer and closer. Four feet, three feet, two feet. He extended his arm and wrapped his hand around her throat. A thought stirred. He knew he couldn't. He looked into her eyes, noticing two different emotions. One was satisfaction, knowing that if he continued, her bargain with Arus would come to fruition. The other emotion he saw was more of something he sensed. It was fear. She was afraid. Eligos knew Marcus all too well, and knew that his sordid past wouldn't stop him from killing her on the spot, regardless of the consequences. But, she noticed his hesitation and her curiosity grew. She narrowed her eyes, as she knew she had the upper hand. "Well," she said, "that's a sensitive topic. I take it he means a great deal to you."

Marcus released his grip reluctantly. He stood face to face with Eligos, trapped between a rock and a hard place. "You demons," he said, "you have no idea what fraternal love is. He is my brother. Obviously not traditionally, but we've bled together. There's no greater bond than that of blood. He is as much my brother as Lucifer is. If you want him, you'll have to get through me first." Eligos slightly smirked.

"You laugh now," Marcus continued, "but I guarantee, you make a threat towards him again, I won't hesitate. Whether I become the Archfiend or not, I will cut you down, purely for the satisfaction. And you know I mean that."

Eligos' demeanour slightly shifted to discomfort. She believed him. Her demise was imminent, were she to pursue her true plan. Her intellect told her to play it safe, and let one of her minions be the one to pay the price. Her task wasn't finished; not yet. She still had much more to accomplish. Eligos was a survivor, and in this moment, her survival instincts kicked in.

She stepped back. "You say that now, but someday soon, you'll be begging me to take it all back. You may be a tougher egg to crack than your father, but at the end of the day, every egg has its weak spot. I will break you. Best you prepare yourself for that day. It fast approaches." She disappeared.

Marcus stood there dumbfounded. His thoughts raced as he couldn't comprehend why she wanted Ben, why Lucas wanted Ben, why Dorian wanted Ben. Obviously it was the fact that he was the Human Angel, and from what had been foretold, Ben having been mentioned in the Revelation, and the fact that he would be involved in the defeat of the bringer of all evil, and leading the armies of Heaven into battle. Again, Marcus had questions. Unsure of his next move, he stood there in deep thought as he slowly turned to look towards the stone that led down to his library. A faint scent once again hit his nose. He raised his head to attune his senses, as the scent was slightly different from Eligos, but not much different. He began to turn around as his leg was grabbed around the ankle, and then another hand wrapped itself tightly around his other ankle. He fell forward as his feet were yanked out from underneath him, and he was pulled from the safety of the consecrated ground. He struggled to grab a hold of the grass in front of him as he was dragged for several feet, whilst hearing sadistic and horrifying screeches and laughter. He then knew exactly what he had sensed.

Marcus fought as much as he could, kicking to try release the grip on his legs as he tried to roll and turn to see his aggressors. He caught a glimpse of the two succubi in their true form, wings and all, with their leathery scaly skin and black eyes that matched their jet black hair. They resembled devils, but under their scaly skin, boasted feminine features. Their skin was a greyish-black, that seemed to have a nacreous sheen, changing shades under different lighting like a pearl does. Both each had a firm grip around his ankles. He kicked one leg free and was able to roll onto his back as he tried to curl forward to grab the hand around his other leg, as the one who had lost her grip on his leg came back and latched on again. They both flew up into the air, hauling him behind them as he opened his golden wings and attempted to fly in the opposite direction. He was much stronger than they were, as they felt themselves being pulled by his sheer strength. It's not that easy to take down a Seraph, even with the element of surprise. But Marcus wasn't just any Seraph, after all, he was the son of Arus.

Marcus aimed for the consecrated ground as suddenly there was another succubus latched onto his arm. Another one swooped in and grabbed his other arm, just as soon as yet another squirmed an arm around his neck. The five of them dragged and pulled as they were only just able to overpower him and began flying back to the ground, away from the chapel. They slammed him onto the dirt and kept as firm a hold as they could, as one slip up, one extremity free, and they'd be done for. He was already angry, and were he to gain the upper hand, the beast in him would be unleashed. They knew all too well what he was capable of, and they had to succeed at all costs. Marcus looked up and saw leathery wings flocking toward him from above; he couldn't count how many succubi were coming toward him, it could have easily been in the hundreds. They swarmed toward him, and all piled on top of him. It was like flies on excrement. The pile grew larger as each of them wanted a piece of him to claim as some sort of gruesome prize. He couldn't just summon his sword. In the position he was in, any one of them could pry it from his hands before he had the chance to do anything. He had to break free. Marcus went limp as he relaxed every muscle in his body. He could feel the claws gouging and scratching as he let his mind slip into itself. It was something he'd done many times before; the calm before the storm. His breathing slowed as he let his rage grow, and he channeled every ounce of strength he had into his arms, legs and back.

Marcus opened his eyes and erupted into a fit of bucking and thrashing as the weight on top of him seemed to get heavier, whilst his open hands scrambled to grab a hold of something, anything he could use. Gaps started to form as the weight dispersed a little more evenly with all his bucking and thrashing, which gave him a little more wiggle room. His right hand closed around something. It was either a wrist or an ankle, he couldn't tell. He just squeezed as he reached with his left hand to find another wrist or ankle; hell, even a neck would do. His left hand found something as he latched on, hard. With all his strength, he yanked his two hands toward each other as hard as he could, bringing one succubi through the mass of their entwined bodies from his right, and the other from his left. They collided in front of him with a mighty thud, after being pulled through God knows how many of their sisters. A gap had formed. He bounced from his back to his feet in one swift kick, still with a strong hold on both succubi. He began flailing them around his head, one by the wrist, and the other by the leg, knocking countless succubi flying. The gap grew larger as he began spinning slowly, still whipping the two back and forth like drumsticks, and he was the crazy drummer. Each succubus he hit was a drum as he felt like every hit was in time with a beat. He tried to guess the tempo as he heard each thud and crack. He guessed 96 beats per minute. Thud, crack, pop, scream, gasp, splash, crash. After all, he was an artist. He finished by snapping them both on the ground like a large finale on the cymbals. Bang! They both hit the ground in unison with such force, the ichor built up inside them and erupted like sweat off the snare drum. He let out a scream which he felt was like a rock scream, but sounded more like a war cry. The succubi were terrified. He looked around almost waiting for applause until he came back to reality and noticed his audience. He wasn't a drummer on stage, he was Marcus. And this was an extermination.

The Sword of the Angels appeared in his hand as a sly smirk appeared across his face. "Who's next, motherfuckers?"

The sword erupted into flames as he darted for the succubus closest to him with the blade sideways. She split in two before bursting, as he swiftly brought the sword around and sliced another backhanded, from waist to shoulder. Marcus began flailing around effortlessly, regardless of his wounds, tearing them apart one by one as they either lunged at him, or retreated in fear. Most stayed, stupidly. They all began to form a large circle around him as they advanced as a unit. Marcus closed his eyes and envisioned the onslaught. His mind filled with countermeasures and tactics as he realised there was no time to waste. He opened his eyes and saw them running toward him, with the circle they had formed getting smaller and smaller in diameter. He went with his instinct and just started slicing. It was what he knew best; spontaneity. There were too many. Once again, they all piled on top of him, but with every ounce of strength, Marcus kept swinging in every direction, trying to cut something, anything. Doom almost seemed to set in, when in a moment, he realised, he would not go out this way. He fought free and swung his sword around more furiously than ever. He was so enthralled by his task, that he didn't even notice the glint of gold in the sky, heading straight for him. His body ached, and his wounds tore as he overexerted every muscle, unwilling to accept his fate. He too, was a survivor. The swarm of succubi seemed to dissipate, as he was noticing less and less targets. Nonetheless, he kept swinging, unable to quash the rage that coursed through every vein in his body, as if the sword had a mind of its own, cutting down everything in its path.

Ichor covered the ground. Marcus was exhausted, but refused to stop. He brought his sword down with two hands in a large overhead swing towards his next target. He stopped, mere millimetres from her face. She looked up at him, her eyes either side of the blade, staring straight into his eyes with pure love. Marcus calmed almost immediately, as he saw Zennah standing in front of him, just underneath his blade. He panted heavily from the exhaustion of battle, and returned her stare, almost feeling sedated as he slowly blinked. Her team of angels were behind her, fiercely disposing of the rest of the succubi. "I had it handled. You didn't have to bring the Valkyrie," Marcus said, almost disappointed.

Zennah half scoffed, half laughed. "Clearly," she said, "Looks like you got in a few lucky punches. I'm intrigued though, was mass genocide on your agenda today?"

Marcus looked around at the ichor on the ground. It was everywhere, like a few dozen dump trucks had reversed and evacuated their loads. His mind wandered through his memory, trying to recall what had just happened. He couldn't remember. Vague recollections popped into his head, but mostly he drew a blank. He shook his head, still in a daze as he looked back at Zennah. "I lost control again, didn't I?"

She put a hand on his cheek lovingly as her thumb caressed his temple and her fingers moved around to the back of his head. She pulled him closer and kissed his forehead as he sunk into the closest feeling he knew to shame. He had felt it before; long ago, after a very dark time in his past. Zennah brought her other hand up to Marcus' face and moved his head to look straight at her, trying to persuade him to keep eye contact. "Talk to me," she said, "You've not been this angry in a long time. Something has you riled up."

Marcus turned and headed for the stone above his library. He opened the stone with his key again, and the ground rumbled as he walked down the stairs again and spoke the same phrase as before, as the stone wall receded. Zennah followed as he stepped back into his library and walked straight past his journals toward an old chest. He tossed his sword up in the air toward its place on the wall as it seemed to glide perfectly into place, and come to rest on the wall, as he knelt in front of the chest. It was a large antique camphor chest, with very detailed etchings around the edge; fine hand carved woodwork, stained a dark brown. There was an untreated pine plank nailed to the top, seemingly as if it were nailed on there to cover up something on the top. The plank had a word carved into it in large block letters. The word was 'DOWNFALL'. He unlocked the chest with the same key that opened the stone to his hidden library, and inside lay some of Marcus' belongings that he hadn't seen in a long time. He took a deep breath that ended with a sigh and pulled out something sitting on the very top. It was a saddle bag, one of a matching pair that used to hang on the side of his saddle. He thought of his old horse, Duke, momentarily; remembering the bond they had, and how the events in Downfall cost Duke his life. Marcus reminisced for a moment longer and put the saddle bag down, noticing that underneath it was a pair of decayed shackles that he had put in there. The shackles were almost a greyish white, as if death itself had touched them, which wasn't too far from the truth.

Marcus shook his head uncomfortably as he discarded the memory and pulled out his gun belt, with large holsters on both sides. It was brown, with plenty of spare bullets in little leather slots most of the way around it. He wrapped it around his waist and latched the belt buckle, whilst tying little pieces of leather string from the bottom of the holsters around his knees. Zennah silently watched as she knew exactly what he was doing; preparing for battle. It was a ritual she had seen many times, and one she knew not to interfere with. He had a task on his mind, his veins still flowed with rage, and to interrupt him now would only cause more chaos. Marcus walked over to the Dragoons sitting in the stand on the shelf and unlatched the cylinder on the gun with the cross on the handle. There were two trays of bullets on the desk; one stack on the left, one stack on the right. They were all hand loaded and pressed by himself, with one minor difference. On each of the bullets on the right was a small cross, carved into each tip, which had each been dipped in holy water. The bullets on the left, they were a lot trickier to make. The process required blue lava from the Flaming River in Hell itself. To create blue lava, you have to burn sulphur in it, and make sure you're in an oxygen rich environment. The outcome of the burning of sulphur turning blue, and melting lead down using blue lava from Hell allows the lead to become cursed. This being poured into moulds and shaped into a bullet tip, could pretty much put down anything. It's deadly to angels, and although less effective against demons, still works some, which is where the blessed bullets come in handy.

Marcus loaded the gun with the cross on the handle with six bullets from the right, and the gun with the pentagram and goats head, he loaded with six bullets from the left. He inspected the gun belt and the bullets in there, making sure there were plenty of each, and then checked the guns themselves to make sure they were in good working condition. They always were, but he liked to make sure. He holstered the two guns and made his way past his sword on the wall. Beyond that was a small hallway, with no exit on the other side. The wall on the left of the hallway was covered with an assortment of weapons, knives, daggers, swords, a mace, a bow, a crossbow, and many others. He took a large combat knife from the wall and found an ankle sheath, which he strapped on and placed the knife in. There was a small vest hanging up on the opposite wall, along with other clothes specifically designed for combat and weapon concealment. The vest had three small throwing knives tucked in each side, like a parody of ribs. All of his weapons had been blessed and soaked in holy water. He took his jacket off and put the vest on, making sure it was well hidden after he put his jacket back on. He didn't mind that the guns were on display. If it truly was Dorian, he wanted to be wearing the very weapon that killed him. He checked himself over, making sure he was armed and ready and walked over to his sword, looking at it fondly, and wondering if it were necessary. He nodded to himself approvingly. After all, it would certainly strike fear in those who opposed him. He left the sword there as he could summon it later, should he need to. He turned around to take another look at the room to see if he'd forgotten anything, and saw Zennah standing there patiently, waiting for him to finish. He had forgotten she was there. "Oh right, you wanted to talk," he said.

Marcus walked over to a chair in front of the table with the bullets, reversed it to face her and sat down. He sat upright, correcting his posture, closed his eyes and breathed deeply. Always part of his ritual. Zennah walked over to him and bent sideways trying to get within his eye line. "Can you stop for a minute, please?" she asked.

Marcus opened his eyes and looked up at her. Her dark hair cascaded beside her face and rested upon her shoulders. Her brown eyes pierced him like daggers, similar to the pair of daggers she had strapped to her belt, that hung down either side of her blue jeans, ripped at the knees. She wore a black leather three quarter coat, over a tight black top, that certainly accentuated her features. Marcus found himself admiring them for a moment. "My eyes are up here, sweetie," she said. He looked up. "I love that you admire my... assets, but you have some explaining to do. What is going on?"

He stared into her eyes deeply, yet with that same blank stare as always. His eyes showed love and adoration for her, but looked straight through her, as his mind raced over the past few weeks. "You remember my friend, Ben? he asked.

"The human?"

"He's the Human Angel."

She gave him a look of confusion, almost a look of disbelief, but with a little reserve. "Okay, you have my attention. I need details. Reasoning behind your thought process."

Marcus rubbed his nose with his thumb, as if scratching an itch, and began to pour over the details of everything that had happened. "He came with me to get my sword, supposedly born to help me find it or something. Turns out he is the descendant of Amalie. The direct descendant."

Zennah nodded. "The first born of the first born. Where the Nephilim bloodline runs strongest. Yet, you've been friends with him for some time. You only just found this out?"

"Yep, this bloodline, it's almost like a curse. Always coming back to haunt me."

"This isn't Downfall, Marcus."

Marcus looked solemnly at the floor. Zennah knew she had hit a nerve. "I'm sorry, I didn't mean to bring it up..."

"You have no idea what happened there."

"So tell me!" she pleaded, "I know it had something to do with that bloodline, otherwise Arus wouldn't have sent you there. Out of everyone you trust, surely I am at least somewhere near the top of that list. Let me help you."

"There's nothing to help. You want to know so badly, read the book. It's on the shelf there."

Zennah frowned at him, trying to move into his line of sight again so he would notice. "I don't want to read it in some fucking book. I want you to tell me, when, or if you're ever ready. You know I'd do anything for you. Hell, I just helped take down a mountain of succubi that just happened to be swarming you for some reason. Bitches got what they deserved in my opinion, trying to get a piece of my man."

Marcus sat up with a recollection that they were discussing Ben. "That's right, Ben."

"He's the Human Angel. How do you know?"

"He became an angel, and his wings turned to yellow!"

She stopped and stared in disbelief. She had her own thoughts on the subject, but she kept them a secret. Her eyes couldn't help but give her away.

"You know something," Marcus said.

Zennah opened her eyes, trying to look nonchalant and confused. "Don't play coy, you're hiding something. Weren't you just ripping through me for the same thing?"

"No, I don't know anything," she lied, "So his wings turned to yellow? Which means he will be a Seraph. Impressive."

Marcus narrowed his eyes on the floor, thinking back to his conversation with Eligos. Zennah noticed the anger start flooding back into him. "What?" she asked.

"They want him."

Fury began to flow through Marcus' veins as his breathing quickened and his blood boiled. His fingers grasped the armrests on the seat he was sitting on as his eyes filled with fire. Zennah instantly grabbed his wrists and wrenched them from the armrests. She rotated his arms to face palm up and began rubbing the inside of his forearms with her thumbs, as she had done many times before to calm him. "Easy there, dragon. Any more anger and flames will shoot out your nose." Marcus snorted a small laugh.

"Close," she said, "but not quite."

He calmed down. "Eligos was here. She said she wants him. Plus Lucas is after him."

"Well, Eligos explains the Succubi. You know better than to dance with her. If you kill her, there's no turning back. Although, she is rather afraid of you."

Marcus shook his head in disagreement. "No," he said, "she isn't. She *wants* me to kill her. She wants to be the one who turned me. She wants her plan to succeed. Not yet, but she wants it."

"All the more reason to avoid her. But Lucas? Now that's interesting. Who would send him after Ben? He's nothing in comparison to you. He always has a master."

"It's Dorian," Marcus said.

"Dorian is dead. You know that better than anyone. It was you who killed him."

"Sam told me. He survived, somehow. That's why I'm here."

"Well that's unheard of. He died in Purgatory in an eruption of flames; they were your exact words from memory. It can't be possible. But, if it is? Now the hundred and fifty year old guns make sense," she said, "Using the very weapon that killed him. Scare tactics, intimidation. I like it."

"I knew you would," Marcus grinned.

"Need help?"

Marcus shook his head. "I have a plan in place. This one, I have to do alone."

Zennah nodded. "Good luck," she said, as she moved forward and kissed him on the lips.

With that, Marcus transported to the alleyway behind Sam's house in Staten Island. The place was in flames and part of the guttering fell to the ground. It seemed there were firemen and police parked out the front, as Marcus could see the blue and red flashing lights coming from above the fence line. He figured it'd be best if he avoided the area all together and began walking towards the hill that Sam had mentioned.

***

Eligos stood in front of Beelzebub in his cavern, as he sat on his throne atop the stony stairs. His body was large and red, with reptile like skin. He had small spikes sticking out of the top of his head like a mohawk, and two large curled horns on either side of his head. His spine was covered in spikes and he had a large tail with spikes forking out of each side. The acrid scent of ichor wafted through from Purgatory as they proceeded with their planning. Beelzebub was concerned that things hadn't been going their way, and he decided to make a power play for Marcus. "He has the sword now, and he and Lucifer are allowed back into Heaven. This is upsetting. We need a win. You need to take him out."

Eligos stood in silence listening to Beelzebub. Her own mind twitched with negativity, as she saw holes in what he wanted to plan. "I believe if I were to pay him another visit, he will proceed with absolute caution, and possibly even flee. No disrespect, but I don't think I'm the one for the job."

Beelzebub stood up, as if he was annoyed by her comment. His eyes shifted to reason as he stepped down one step. "You may be right. We need someone he won't expect, and someone he wouldn't be afraid to get close to."

"I believe I can be of assistance." The voice came from the entrance. A figure waddled in, half demon, half in human form. It was Percy. The human side of his face was scarred badly, and the demon half had a big, black menacing eye. Hair flowed down his good side below his ears; thin and wispy, and dead straight. His clothing was tattered and stained, and his feet were covered in ichor. Beelzebub sat down and leaned forward, glaring at Percy, unimpressed that he was leaving muddy footprints on the floor. A slight devilish grin cracked on his face as his mind wandered. He knew of Percy's history with Marcus, and knew that Marcus wouldn't trust him, but also knew that Percy was cunning, and would take any chance he could get. "On one condition, though," Percy added.

Beelzebub sat back and relaxed. "Freedom?"

"Full freedom, power back and all. And preferably a full face."

Beelzebub nodded. "I'll give you power now; you'll need it against him. You can have your human form back once you deliver him here."

Percy grinned evilly. "Consider it done."

***

Marcus walked up the hill on a dimly lit street, which had mostly large houses on it, only the one at the top of the hill was the largest. Marcus looked up at the large house as he kept walking. He had determination in his eyes and a maniacal half smile on his face. He was puffing on a cigarette and began walking faster. He stopped dead as his senses filled with a feeling. Something was very wrong. It wasn't a scent, it wasn't a taste, it was almost a shiver. Something from his past that he'd tried desperately to forget. He dropped his cigarette. His breathing slowed as he considered what to do, and a figured emerged out of nothingness, shrouded in black and grabbed his jacket. The two of them were instantly standing in the ethereal realm. The ethereal realm is on the same plane as the corporeal realm, it is just unseen to the naked eye. The corporeal realm is the world as we know it.

Everything glowed in a slightly grayscale tone, almost as if everything were in black and white, but with very slight hues of browns. It was where ethereal beings lived. Ghosts, ghouls. What the Heaven and Hell referred to as Apparitions. Beyond the shrouded figure were four more figures, all on spectral horses. Their faces were a ghastly white, like skulls, but with no muscle, just skin stretched over it. Their mouths weren't one large opening, the skin stretched in parts between the upper and lower, leaving small gaps, like the front grill of a car. There was a sunken black hole where the nose would normally be, and glowing eyes behind black, skull-like eye sockets. The figure holding onto Marcus' jacket lifted its head to reveal the same face. Marcus looked at the four figures behind on their horses, which all had their own colour. One was red, one was black, one was green, and one was pale. In between the four horsemen was a fifth horse; riderless - obviously belonging to the figure holding onto Marcus. The figure let go of Marcus and stood back almost like he'd just performed a magic trick, which in a sense, it kind of was. He had pulled Marcus from the corporeal realm, into the ethereal realm, and generally in crossing over, you end up geographically in the same place. They weren't in the same place. They had been transported at the same time, to somewhere in the middle of Washington state. Marcus recognised the countryside around him instantly. Beyond the horsemen was a sword sticking out of the ground, glowing fiercely, emitting some kind of dome. Inside the dome, was a town; a small town, that looked to be built in the nineteenth century; a town that no longer existed in the corporeal realm.

Downfall.

Of the four horsemen, from left to right, was War, Famine, Pestilence, and Death. What was commonly unknown, is that there was a fifth. Although he wasn't the fifth. He was the first, and he was the strongest of them all.

Conquest.

Conquest stepped back and mounted his white spectral horse in the middle of the others as Marcus just stared. His eyes weren't quite looking at them, but through them, and resting on the sword that shielded the enclosed town of Downfall behind them. It was a place he hadn't seen in well over a century, and a place that still haunted him. The luminescent dome was a powerful circumscribe, placed by God himself, so that no one could go in, and no one could get out. The town was sealed within it, and trapped in the ethereal realm forever. It could be unsealed, but only by someone very powerful. An angel. They would have to be a Seraph. But there was a catch. They had to have also been human. Marcus had once been human, technically, for a time. Conquest had killed him, and he ended up in Purgatory, powerless; basically, a human. But, Marcus escaped. Something that hadn't been achieved by any being, without making a deal for their release. If escape were successful, crossing the gates of Heaven or Hell would restore their angelic or demonic power. Marcus, having being banished from Heaven, was unable to cross the gates and restore his power. He had to live for a time, as a human. It was the reason he had free will.

Apart from the horsemen, there were only two that knew Marcus had escaped. One was Gabriel, the other was God himself. Marcus continued to stare as Death dismounted his horse and walked toward him. Marcus took his gaze away from Downfall and looked into the fiery red glowing eyes of Death as a sudden realisation hit him. This wasn't a social visit. Out of the five horsemen, Death was the only one that Marcus didn't actually despise. Death took human form, showing the features of a seasoned man, with skin like leather, and silvery white hair, dressed all in black. It was the same outfit Marcus had seen him wearing over a century ago, in the very town that lay just behind the horsemen. Black coat, with a black waistcoat, and a grey shirt. His pale eyes gave off a little emotion that Marcus picked up on straight away. "It's my time, isn't it?" he asked.

Death slowly nodded as Marcus looked back up at the other horsemen. "So, what are they doing here?"

Death stepped beside Marcus and put a hand on his back to signal him to walk. Marcus obliged as they veered around the horsemen toward Downfall. Marcus grew uneasy as it felt like his past coming back to haunt him. Death started to speak. "We came to bargain. You have a very daunting task ahead of you, and you could use our help."

Marcus began to frown. "Why would I want your help?" he scoffed.

"Bygones be bygones, Marcus. We don't hold a grudge. All you need to do, is open the town. Let us retrieve our essences, so that we may be what we once were. You possess the Rescinder Blade, the only weapon capable of killing us, ergo, we are under your command."

"Didn't do me a lot of good back in Downfall."

Death turned around to face him. "We had an agenda, back then. Now, we just want to get back on the horse, so to speak. No pun intended."

Marcus looked at the town in front of him, shrouded within the dome; faces pressed hard up against it. One hundred and twelve people, all staring out at him with blank expressionless eyes; the essence of all five horsemen trapped within them, consuming them. They were no longer who they once were. They got sick, they starved, they went to war with each other, and then they died. But, shortly after that, they rose, with the essence of Conquest. With only one agenda; to conquer. Marcus barely made it out alive. He looked away in shame. "You feel guilt." Death said.

"Why shouldn't he?" Conquest said, as he dismounted his white horse. He had changed into his human form, which was known once as Winston Thacker, Marshal of Klickitat County; the very place Downfall once stood. His suit was all white, with a wide brim white hat placed on top of his face. His hair was white, slightly poking out at the sides of the hat, obviously parted in the middle, and a moustache and beard, trimmed to a fine point below his chin. He walked over to them. "He did this," he said.

Marcus stood up tall and opened his golden wings. His moment of weakness had passed, and Conquest had pissed him off. "You should have left Death to do the talking. He might have convinced me, but I know you're pulling the strings. You don't want to help me; you just want your essence back. That will make all five of you the strongest beings that ever lived. You'll all be unstoppable." Marcus smirked. "Well, almost unstoppable. Don't forget, I was practically human last time. Powerless. And I still killed all five of you. See the wings? What do you think I'd do to you, now that you're powerless?"

Conquest grabbed Marcus by the jacket again. "Don't threaten me, boy. You open that town, we get our essences back, we help you with your impending doom, and possibly a few extras, and then we can be on our way."

Marcus nodded. "On your way, to consume humanity as we know it. There's only about eight billion people out there. I'm not having that on my conscience. I'd rather die."

"Then so be it!" Conquest barked as he turned around and walked back to his horse.

Marcus looked up at Death who wasn't thrilled with the turn of events, as he returned Marcus' stare. "Sorry Marcus, there's nothing more I can do. You've sealed your fate."

Marcus nodded. He understood. "So be it," he said.

Death put a hand on his shoulder as Marcus was instantly standing back in the corporeal realm, by himself. The town of Downfall was gone, and so were the horsemen. He breathed a sigh of relief, which was also mixed with acceptance. He knew what he had to do, he knew what it would cost him, and he knew that he deserved it. In his final tasks, all he hoped was that it would somehow redeem his actions, all those years ago. He transported back to his apartment and fumbled around on the coffee table for pen and paper. He found a yellow post it note and a pen, and wrote a phrase on it.

Ben, the blade that takes back, that annuls, revokes.

Below that, he wrote a word in Hebrew, hoping that when the time came, Ben would get the reference and be able to figure it out.

ארון

It was the very same word that was on the wall of the Chislehurst Caves. He figured that if it were true that his time was up, and he were to fall, Ben would eventually get around to reading his journals. He trusted him enough to allow him to find the library, should he be able to figure out the note. He took the key from his pocket and placed it back in the Ethiopia book along with the note. Marcus set off once again for the house at the top of the hill. He transported back to the street and reached the top of the hill, and walked past the large spiked fence and in through the open gate in the middle. The two storey house ahead of him was large and made of a brown sort of stone. It looked like an old spooky mansion, with a big entrance porch with two big pillars on either side, and either side of the entrance way the house panned out almost to the end of the fence line. He stopped and looked up at it with a hint of hesitation, then walked up to the front door and slammed the side of his fist against it twice. The large double doors moved as he banged his hand against them and made a large booming noise, almost as if the noise was echoing off the empty corridors inside. He heard quiet footsteps getting louder; a dress shoe on wooden floorboards. The sound was almost hypnotic, and with each step, the sound grew louder and louder. The old door creaked and opened all the way. There was a large man standing in the doorway in a suit. He looked down at Marcus and stood back. "Can I help you?" the man asked.

"Tell Dorian that Marcus is here," Marcus said.

"Wait here please." The man closed the door and walked down the large corridor towards the door at the end of the hallway. He opened it and walked into a large room with a long dining table running across it. There were about twelve men sitting at the table. Dorian was on the end to the man's right, and at a right angle next to him was Lucas. "A Marcus here to see you, sir," the man said.

Dorian stood up at the head of the table and looked mystified at his servant. He shifted his eyes to all the men sitting at the table around him and then back at the servant. "Marcus is here?" he asked. The servant nodded. "Curious, send him in."

The servant walked out the door and down the large corridor to the front door. He opened up the front door for Marcus and stood aside. "Please go right on in, sir," the servant said.

Marcus stepped inside the door as the servant closed it quietly. Marcus looked around at the large corridor and then looked at the servant. He stepped a little closer to him and looked him up and down. "Human," he said, "let's hope you know what you're dealing with."

The servant walked down the corridor towards the door at the end, while Marcus followed him. They walked into the large room and Marcus saw the men all sitting at the table, and Dorian standing at the end with his fists resting on the table. He looked around the room and saw paintings on the wall of families; the pictures all looked like different generations of the same blood line. He noticed a large painting of Dorian on the wall right behind the head of the table where Dorian stood. His eyes moved back down to Dorian. "Marcus!" Dorian shouted, "It's been years since I last saw you. Where was it again?"

"Purgatory. With my blade in your arm," Marcus said as he looked around the room. "And my gun in your mouth, as you burst into flames."

"Ah yes," Dorian said, "that's right. I remember now. You know it seems so long ago."

"One does have to wonder how you survived," Marcus said.

"Oh I didn't survive. I will admit you did your job very well," Dorian replied.

"Well based on this conversation, I'd have to disagree. How did you do it?" Marcus asked.

"That, my friend, is a secret," Dorian said.

"I'm not your friend. And you can't keep secrets from me. I believe that's what got you killed in the first place," Marcus said.

"Right you are," Dorian said. He wasn't a tall man, but he had broad shoulders and a large square jaw. His hair was brown and parted in the middle with his fringe hanging almost over his eyes. "So, what can I do for you?" he asked.

"You can leave Ben alone."

The men around the table all laughed, except for Lucas who had his gaze fixed on Marcus. Marcus returned his stare. "In case you were wondering," Dorian said, "that was a no."

"Wrong answer," Marcus said.

"Oh no, I think it was the right answer. For you see, this is my house. I inherited it from my family. And in my house, you are powerless. The only power that works in here, boy, is evil."

"Then I'm sure there's another way we can settle this," Marcus said.

"And how do you propose we do that?" Dorian asked.

Marcus extended his arm and pointed at Lucas. "I fight him," Marcus said, "Hand to hand combat, no power, and if I win, you leave Ben alone."

"And what if he wins?" Dorian asked.

Marcus held his arms out beside him with a small shrug. "You get me," he said, "What you've always wanted." Marcus looked over at Lucas. "The very reason he exists."

Dorian let the words sink in as he stared at the floor in front of Marcus. His eyes were flicking back and forth in a stare as if he was weighing up the odds. He looked up at Marcus with a smile and nodded. "You've got a deal, my friend," Dorian said.

"I told you, I'm not your fucking friend," Marcus replied.

Lucas stood up and walked towards the back wall. He took off his black jacket and dumped it onto the floor. He was wearing a tight black t-shirt underneath and had a tribal-like tattoo running down the inside of his forearm. He turned around and faced the table as Marcus walked around it. He unzipped his jacket and threw it onto the ground and took his vest off, placing it on top of his jacket. He then pulled his blue t-shirt up over his head. He threw it on the ground on top of his vest and jacket, then took off his gun belt and went to drop it on his jacket. He thought twice, thinking he didn't want the guns to fall into the wrong hands, so he held the belt in his hand and let it disappear. Lucas tilted his head to the side to crack his neck and clenched his fists. Marcus rubbed his palm again and stood front on to Lucas. They stared at each other for a long minute, assessing the situation and wondering what the other would do. Lucas darted forward and charged at Marcus. He put his head down and his arms out, ready to tackle Marcus to the ground. *Big mistake,* Marcus thought, as he turned side on, lowered his head and threw his shoulder into Lucas' chest, stopping his momentum, as he wrapped his left leg lightly behind Lucas' and tripped him over. They both fell to the floor and Marcus put his elbow into Lucas' throat. Lucas kicked him off and jumped to his feet. He disappeared for a second and came up behind Marcus and wrapped his arm around his throat. "I said no power," Marcus struggled to say.

He grabbed Lucas by the arm and reached his other arm over his head, grabbing hold of the back of Lucas' neck. He flipped Lucas over the top of him and threw him onto the floor at his feet. Lucas was sprawled on his back with his head just in between Marcus' feet. Marcus put his right foot just under Lucas' left arm and rolled himself around and underneath it, with both his legs either side of Lucas' arm. He pushed his legs down on Lucas' chest and pulled his hand back, bending the elbow. Lucas still had his strength and was able to do a bicep curl to pull against the strain, but even without his power, Marcus was strong. They held themselves there in a stalemate, as Lucas channeled all his strength into his arm and wrenched Marcus forward, then swung his right arm around to punch him in the face. Marcus lost his grip and Lucas rolled over onto his front and jumped up to his feet again. Marcus stood up and stepped forward and grabbed hold of Lucas' t-shirt and with his other hand, grabbed hold of Lucas' shoulder. He fell backwards and into a roll, still holding onto Lucas, and pushed his foot into Lucas' stomach, launching him over his head.

Marcus stood up and dusted off his jeans. He turned around as Lucas tackled him to the floor. Lucas began punching Marcus in the face over and over again. Blood started pouring out of Marcus' nose. Lucas stopped for a second to inspect the damage as Marcus grabbed him around the throat and threw him sideways. Marcus leapt up to his feet in one quick bounce. He wiped the blood off his face and shook his hand to flick it onto the floor. He walked up to Lucas and grabbed him around the throat with both hands and began squeezing hard. Lucas grabbed Marcus' wrists and wrenched them apart, head butting Marcus in the face. Marcus staggered backwards while Lucas leapt forward with a mighty kick to the chest. Marcus fell to the ground. He shuffled onto his hands and knees and slowly stood up. As he looked up, Lucas was lunging forward with his leg extended, coming fast. The large, black boot hit Marcus in the face, and he fell sideways into the wall and collapsed on the floor. Lucas clenched in shock as he celebrated silently. His closed fists came up near his face to hide a small smile of triumph. He relaxed and breathed a sigh of relief as Dorian walked past him and gave him a pat on the shoulder. Dorian then walked over to Marcus and looked him up and down. He was unconscious and barely breathing. Dorian put his hand on Marcus' forehead and Marcus began convulsing. "Now you're my friend," Dorian chuckled to himself.

***

Ben was in the training room with Michael and Lucifer, and they were both coming at him with everything they had. Ben had the staff as he was swatting them away like they were nothing; blocking, dodging, ducking, and striking. He constantly knocked both of them over with ease, and each time, they came back with even more ferocity. Ben's wings were open, and as he continued with what seemed to be an endless battle, his wings began glowing brighter and brighter. But, they just wouldn't turn to complete gold. Ben was frustrated. He called a time out. "Let's bring in another two angels. This isn't working," he said.

Michael shook his head. "Honestly, I don't think that will help. We're almost there, but it just doesn't seem to be working. I can't figure out why."

"I know why," Lucifer said. He let his sword disappear and sat down with exhaustion. Michael turned his head sideways, trying to figure it out. Lucifer caught his breath and looked up at the two of them. "He can beat us until we're blue in the face, but there's only one he has to beat to get his gold wings."

Michael nodded. "You're right. The one who trained him."

Ben stood up straight. Confusion hit his eyes. "But you're training me, doesn't it work that way?"

"It's you who's stopping it," Michael said, "You believe that you won't be good enough until you truly defeat Marcus in combat, as you see him as the strongest. It's your mind that's challenging you."

God walked in the room and up to where Ben and Lucifer were standing. They both looked up at him. "Something has happened to Marcus," he said.

Lucifer and Ben both looked at each other, then at Michael, and then back at God in unison. "What?" Ben asked.

"Go to help him," God said.

"Where is he?" Lucifer asked.

"He is where he told you he would be."

Lucifer remembered Marcus telling him that it was near Sam's place. He remembered him saying the old mansion on the hill. "Let's go," Ben said.

"I can't, you're not ready yet. Marcus told me not to bring you until you're ready," Lucifer said.

"I don't care! I'm ready enough!" Ben shouted, "He'd do it for me, and I am not going to just sit back and wait."

Lucifer almost cowered before Ben. He certainly looked at Ben with a new respect. "Okay, to be honest, he did say almost ready. Are you sure you're confident in your transporting?" Lucifer asked.

"I'll be fine," Ben said.

"Okay, meet me out the back of Sam's place," Lucifer said, and disappeared.

Ben looked at God. "Am I ready for this?" he asked.

"You have learnt a lot Ben, but only *you* can know if you are truly ready for this," God said.

Ben nodded. "God, please give me the strength to do this." God put his hand on Ben's shoulder, and he smiled and turned to walk back up the steps.

Ben looked at Michael. "Was that it? Did he give me the strength? Or was that just a comforting gesture?" Ben asked.

Michael shrugged. "You'll know when the time comes, I guess."

Ben half frowned. "Thanks for the reassurance." He transported away, and found himself standing out the front of Sam's house. The house had burnt to the ground, and a smell of water and smoke filled his nostrils. Ben stepped back and bumped into Lucifer. "What happened here?" he asked.

"Marcus had him killed," Lucifer replied.

Ben stared at the rubble. "Why?" he asked.

"Because you don't lie to Marcus," Lucifer explained, "Come on."

They walked briskly towards the hill at the end of the street and saw the mansion on top. They made their way around to the actual street the house was on and Lucifer took off quickly up towards the top. Ben followed him instantly. They powered up the hill past the houses on either side and Lucifer stopped. He held his arm out in front of Ben to stop him as well. Eligos was standing in front of them. Between them and the house. She looked at Lucifer. "Nice night for a stroll," she said.

"What do you want?" Lucifer asked.

Eligos ignored the question and looked directly at Ben. "You must be Ben," she said.

Ben stepped back, a little discomforted. Lucifer tried to stand slightly in front of Ben to shield him. Eligos became amused. "Please, I'm not afraid of you. Your brother, on the other hand, that's a different story. He wouldn't hesitate, regardless of consequences. You've got too much to lose now. I could pluck him from you, and you'd just have to sit there and watch."

Eligos edged slightly closer, and Lucifer pulled his sword. "Stay back!" he shouted.

She didn't stop. "You can't kill me either, remember?"

A flash of gold landed in between them with a mighty thud as Arus straightened himself up and stood tall, with his sword, Beast in his right hand. Both Lucifer and Ben were dumbfounded. Arus looked Eligos squarely in the eyes. "But, I can," he said. Eligos grimaced and returned his stare, but Arus didn't budge. "You stay away from my boys. All of them."

Ben clued on. He realised it was Arus, and a small, boyish smile fell across his face. Arus considered him a part of the family. Eligos disappeared. Arus turned around to face Ben and Lucifer who were still staring at him like he was from another planet. "Well?" he said, "Go!"

They walked past Arus and in through the gate and up to the front door. Ben slammed the side of his fist against the door, and they heard footsteps coming towards them. It almost seemed like they were waiting forever when the door finally opened. The servant was standing there looking at the two of them. "Can I help you?" the servant asked.

"We're here to see Dorian," Lucifer said.

"And you are?" the servant asked.

"Lucifer and Ben," Lucifer said.

The servant looked puzzled. He shrugged and closed the door, and Lucifer and Ben listened to his footsteps recede down the hallway inside. "Will they let us in?" Ben asked.

"I hope so," Lucifer replied.

They heard the footsteps coming towards the front door again, and waited in anticipation until the door finally opened. "Please go right on in, gentlemen," the servant said.

Ben and Lucifer walked in and followed the servant down the corridor to the door at the end. As they walked through the door, they looked at the large table and all the men sitting around it. Dorian was standing at the head of the table to their right with his fists resting on the table. "Lucifer, what a pleasant surprise," Dorian said. He shifted his gaze over to Ben. "And you must be Ben," he said.

"How are you still breathing?" Lucifer asked.

Dorian gave a small chuckle. "You know, it's really quite funny. I asked your brother that very same question only minutes ago."

Ben closed his eyes and let an image fill his mind. It was an image of him pulling his new sword out from under his jacket, just like Marcus does. He reached under his jacket and believed that it would happen and successfully pulled his sword out from under his jacket and stepped forward. "Where is he?" he shouted.

"Somebody has a temper. He's right over there," Dorian said. Ben and Lucifer looked past the table and saw Marcus lying on the floor. They ran around the table just in time to see him standing up. He faced the wall as he stood up and brushed his jeans, leaning down to pick up his jacket. He pulled out a packet of cigarettes and threw his jacket back on the ground, pulling one out of the packet and a lighter out of his pants pocket. He put the cigarette in his mouth and lit it, then threw the lighter and the packet on top of his jacket. He turned around to face Ben and Lucifer and they stood back as they saw his eyes. They were completely black. He looked over at Dorian. "Kill them," Dorian said.

Marcus' wings began to seep out of his back. They were no longer gold, but black. They grew up above his head and formed sharp points as Marcus began walking towards Ben. Ben's own wings began to seep out of his back. They were still a green gold colour and Marcus watched them rise up into the air. Marcus' sword appeared in his hand and he put his left foot back ready to fight. "Marcus, it's me. It's Ben!" Ben shouted.

"I don't think that's Marcus anymore," Lucifer said. Ben looked over at Dorian, while Lucifer kept his eyes on Marcus. Marcus blinked and his eyes flashed blue for a second and then faded back to black. He winked at Lucifer. Lucifer raised an eyebrow and half smiled as his sword appeared in his hand. "Ben, fight him," Lucifer said.

Marcus lunged at Ben with the sword, but Ben blocked it with his own sword. Marcus swung again and Ben jumped backwards to avoid being hit. He circled around Marcus and held his stare. His eyes were big and black and filled with anger. He swung at Ben again and Ben knocked Marcus' sword sideways. He stood back. "I don't want to hurt him," Ben said to Lucifer.

"That's really funny," Marcus said, "*You*, hurt *me*?" He pulled his sword all the way above his head and hurled it down towards Ben's head. Ben fell to his knee and held his sword across his face. Marcus' sword hit Ben's with a mighty clang. Ben stepped up and forward, and kicked Marcus in the stomach. Marcus stumbled backwards. He came at Ben again, but Ben quickly turned around and slapped the flat of the blade on Marcus' back. Marcus fell forward and onto the ground. His sword fell out of his hands and skidded across the floor. He rolled onto his back and looked up at Ben and saw Ben's sword an inch away from his face. Marcus looked up at Ben as his wings turned from green gold, to full gold.

Marcus half smiled and stood up. He walked over to his sword and picked it up. His dagger quickly appeared in his other hand. He turned and threw it at Dorian, hitting him just above the chest. Dorian staggered back and fell over his chair. Marcus flew up into the air and landed on the end of the table at the other end. The men sitting at the table all stood up and let their black leathery wings seep out of their backs. Marcus walked along the table and with both hands, sliced the first man in half. He turned around and decapitated the man opposite. His movements were as fast as lightning, and the men at the table almost didn't have time to react. They lunged at him all at once, leaping onto the table as Marcus let his sword disappear as one came up on his left and swung at him. He leaned back so that the punch would miss, and the man's arm travelled too far past his mark. He was now side on to Marcus, with his right arm still travelling through the large arc. Marcus leaned back in quickly, and grabbed the hair on the back of the man's head. He bent him over backwards and landed a colossal blow, right to his face. The man fell down as Marcus' elbow instantly started travelling in the opposite direction and hit one of the men straight in the cheek bone. They kept coming.

Ben was in awe, watching Marcus take on several men with his bare hands, and toss them around like they were weightless. Every blow, every hit, Ben studied hard; mimicking as he always did, to learn. He had now understood when Ryan told him he'd seen him take on seven men. Marcus was unbeatable. A flash of fire appeared as Marcus had re-summoned his sword and began cutting them down, one by one. He made his way to the very end of the table, leaving a trail of ichor behind him. He stopped right in front of Lucas and stared at him with his large black eyes. Lucas stood up out of his chair and stumbled backwards, scraping the chair across the floor. Lucas looked up at Marcus with the realisation that he had only won the fight because Marcus had let him. He had used his power in the fight and Marcus hadn't been able to, yet Marcus wasn't even fighting to his full potential. He was only losing the fight to gain the use of power in the house. Lucas fell to his knees and bowed his head, admitting defeat. Marcus jumped down off the table and walked up to Lucas. He stood right in front of him and looked down. Lucas lifted his head up and looked into Marcus' eyes. "You are nothing like me. I never admit defeat," Marcus said.

Lucas lowered his head again. Marcus shifted his hands around the handle of his sword so that it was below the knuckles. He raised it above Lucas and thrust it through his back. Lucas burst into a puddle of ichor. Marcus stood upright and let his sword disappear as he walked around the head of the table to where Dorian was lying on the floor gasping. He knelt on top of him and pulled the dagger out, and stabbed it straight back in again. Dorian groaned in pain. "How did you do it?" Marcus asked.

"Do what?" Dorian struggled to ask.

"How did you come back? Tell me!" he shouted. Marcus pulled the dagger out and stabbed it back in again, as Dorian groaned again. "Tell me!"

"I don't know, I don't know!" Dorian screamed.

"Don't lie to me!" Marcus shouted.

His eyes were crazy. His teeth were clenched shut in absolute rage as he spoke through them. He had his hand wrapped firmly around the handle of the dagger sticking out of Dorian's chest, as he was glaring at into his eyes, waiting for an answer. Dorian looked into his crazed eyes and saw something he'd never seen in those eyes before. Fear. The penny dropped. Dorian realised why Marcus was asking. He managed to bring a small smirk to his face. "You don't just want to know. Your time is up, isn't it?" he whispered.

Marcus' eyes filled with more fury as he pulled the dagger out and stabbed him again several times. Dorian screamed and groaned with each new wound, until he found himself laughing. It hurt him, but he couldn't resist. Seeing Marcus in a frenzy of fear was a delight that almost made the pain bearable. His suit was covered in his blood as it oozed out of each wound, and he struggled to lift his head closer to Marcus' ears. "Good luck," he slyly said.

Marcus' lip twitched as he picked him up by his bloody suit and stared into his eyes. "Stay dead this time," he said.

The room around them disappeared and they were surrounded by decaying bodies. Angels and demons surrounded them, watching. Marcus dumped Dorian onto the ichor covered ground. He pulled his dagger out of Dorian's chest and let his sword appear as he instantly thrust it right through him. Dorian screamed in pain and burst into flames once again, as he disintegrated to ash and melted away into the wet ground. Marcus found himself standing back in the room with the large dining table and was looking down at the floor. He turned and looked at Ben and Lucifer. He let his sword disappear and closed his eyes as he shook his head violently, and when he opened his eyes, they were blue again. He looked up at his wings and gave them a mighty flick. All of the black flew off of them and they turned back to gold. He looked at Ben and Lucifer again. "Oh good, he's back," Ben said.

Marcus looked away uncomfortably and breathed heavily to try and calm himself. He rolled his shoulders and turned back toward them. "That was your plan all along, wasn't it? Becoming bad, fighting Ben," Lucifer asked.

"There's a lesson in that for you. Being bad is sometimes being good," Marcus said.

They laughed. Marcus looked up at Ben's gold wings floating above him. "Nice wings," he said.

Ben looked up and saw his gold wings floating above him. He looked at Marcus and smiled. "They're gold!" he said.

"That, they are," Marcus said, "Come on, I need a drink."

"Hang on," Lucifer said, "I'm going to take a look around."

Lucifer walked around the room and then moved through a doorway to investigate the rest of the house. Ben was looking at the large table covered in ichor with a thought racing through his mind. Marcus was a skilled warrior, but such fire burned through him. It couldn't just be his training; something had happened to him that had caused him to be that way. Something terrible. It had to be whatever Downfall was. He remembered seeing the missing book from the bookshelf in Marcus' apartment, and his change in behaviour at the mere mention of the word. It was something Marcus was afraid of, and anything that Marcus was afraid of, scared Ben to death. "Hey, Marcus?"

Marcus was putting his shirt, vest and jacket back on. "What's up?" Marcus replied.

Ben wasn't sure how to ask. He knew it was a touchy subject, but he needed to know. "What happened in Downfall?"

Marcus stopped. His mood instantly changed; only this time it was different. It wasn't anger, like the last time. It wasn't fear. It was more of a sadness. Almost a look of guilt. Ben instantly picked it. "What happened, man?" Ben asked again.

Marcus shook his head. "No. I can't."

"Why not? It obviously bothers you. You can talk to me. I just watched you take all of those guys out with pure rage. That wasn't just training. There's something that created that flame inside of you. I think it's whatever happened in Downfall. You can confide in me."

"Why are you so obsessed with finding out?" Marcus barked.

"Because there's something out there that you're afraid of!" Ben shouted back. Marcus stood still for a long moment, and Ben broke the silence. "If there's something out there that you're afraid of, then that scares the shit out of me. I'm becoming one of you guys, I'm gonna need to know what's really out there, so I can help you fight it. I want to know, so that when the time comes, I'll be equipped with knowledge."

Marcus remained still and silent, just staring. The memories flooded back. The town, the horsemen, his friend Keme, who was of the Blackfoot tribe. One hundred and twelve dead, one survivor. One who Marcus had helped escape before the events there unfolded; a man by the name of Hugh Mitchell, who moved to Huntington, New York, and changed his last name to Waters. The bloodline. Marcus thought back to his recent meeting with the horsemen, and their attempt to try bargain with him; wanting him to open Downfall to retrieve their essence; the catastrophe that would follow, were they re-empowered. The fifth seal of the Apocalypse. The Altar of Souls. The souls of martyrs being released to claim vengeance on those who martyred them. It was imperative that the fifth seal not be opened. It was imperative that the horsemen did not regain their essence. The town of Downfall could only be opened by a Seraph, who was human at a time. Ben was human, Ben was now a Seraph. Ben could open Downfall if they were able to persuade him. Ben needed to know the truth, which was why Marcus left the key and the note in the book back in his apartment for Ben to find. Marcus stood there in his quiet contemplation as Ben grew tired of his silence. "Marcus!" Ben shouted.

Marcus awoke from his stupor and looked at Ben, almost forgetting he was there. He opened his mouth to speak, but only one thought came to mind. "And I heard a voice, in the midst of the four beasts. And I looked, and behold. A pale horse." Marcus struggled and breathed heavily. "And his name that sat upon him, was Death." Marcus stopped at the next sentence, as it was the hardest part to say. It was the part that rang truest for him, and the part that scared him the most. Ben's eyes were wide open, as he listened intently. Marcus opened his mouth and began to shiver. "And hell followed with him..."

Ben took a deep breath. He knew the passage. He knew what it referenced, but he still had questions. "That's Revelations. That's... That's the four horsemen. The four horsemen were in Downfall?"

Marcus blinked and slowed his breathing as he looked at the floor. "Five. There's five of them."

"But I thought they were on our side. Weren't they created by God for..." Ben realised, "oh shit".

Marcus nodded and Ben saw the connection. "How many people?" he asked.

Marcus breathed in and out heavily. "One hundred and twelve."

Ben dropped his jaw. He was dumbfounded. He completely understood. Not being able to save that many people would cripple anyone. It wasn't something he was afraid of; it was what he failed. He was ashamed. Lucifer walked back in. "I'd be almost tempted to take this place as my own. This is a palace," he said.

Marcus and Ben shifted to hide their discomfort. Lucifer noticed. "What's going on in here?" he asked.

"Nothing," Ben said, "Just making sure we have all our bases covered."

"Well, on that note, mission accomplished. Let's go."

The servant walked into the room and looked at the mess around the table. "What happened in here?" he asked.

"Something you'll never talk about again. Congratulations, you just became the sole owner of this house," Marcus said. They walked down the corridor and out the front door. The servant stared at the mess in the room. He grabbed his head and fell to his knees in pain. His eyes started bulging as something tried to enter his mind. He didn't know what was happening, but whatever it was, it didn't feel good. One of his eyes turned black, as that side of his body began to turn a deep shade of red.

As they 'walked down the steps outside the front door, Marcus stopped, as Eligos was standing near the gate. His anger renewed as he began to walk toward her confidently, and swapped his sword into his left hand. She noticed his demeanour and held her hands out in front, almost intimidated. "Now, Marcus. Wait a minute, darling. I'm just here to talk."

Marcus sneered, "I'm done talking. I don't care anymore". He lunged forward and landed a huge blow to the left side of her face as she fell sideways. She regained her balance and held her face. It hurt. Lucifer and Ben looked on in shock, especially Lucifer. He didn't understand why Marcus was so unhinged, and being so careless. He hadn't been able to hear what Dorian was saying, as he was whispering. Whatever it was, it mustn't have been pleasant, especially with Dorian laughing. Marcus stood there, full of rage, as Eligos feared for her life. She no longer wanted to threaten him, she no longer wanted to toy with him. He wasn't playing the game anymore. He was just going to kill her. Either this time, or the next, or the next. She could leave with her life, but he would come for her. The huntress had become the hunted. She was marked for death. She retreated, as Marcus stood and watched her go. Ben and Lucifer walked up behind him and watched. "You know dude, you should never hit a lady."

Marcus glared at Ben. "A lady would never make me want, or need to. I would never raise my hand to a lady. That, was no lady. That, was a demon."

Ben looked at Lucifer, who nodded and shrugged in a sort of agreement. "She is a demon; she's put us all through hell." Ben shrugged. Angels, demons, he was slowly getting used to it. They walked out of the gate and began walking down the street when they heard a manic, hysterical screaming laugh coming from the house. They all turned around to look at the house. The laugh died away.

"Oh no," Marcus said.

"What is it?" Ben asked.

"Percy," Marcus and Lucifer said.

They ran back through the gate and up to the front door. Marcus turned the handle and pushed it open. The three of them ran down the corridor and into the large room at the end and stopped dead as they got through the door. The room was exactly how they left it, and the chandelier on the roof above the table was slightly rocking from side to side. Marcus stepped further into the room and looked all around it, and walked around the long table to where he'd fought

Lucas. "Come on out Percy, I think we need to talk," Marcus said.

"Talking, that's all you ever do," a voice said. Marcus turned a full circle and still didn't see anybody. "Talk and drink," the voice continued.

"Unfortunately for you, this time I am stone sober. How did you get out?" Marcus asked.

The voice laughed. It sounded like it was coming from behind the end wall. "Wouldn't you like to know?" the voice giggled.

"Show yourself. I never thought you'd be so cowardice to hide from me."

A section of the back wall began opening. It was like a secret door that had no handle on the outside. Percy was standing in the doorway with his brown, straight hair sticking out of his head and flowing down one side of his face. The other side of his face was glaring at them with his large black eye. He bounced into the room, almost like he was dancing. He had a smile on the human side of his face. "What did you offer Beelzebub?" Marcus asked, "because I know you didn't kill him."

Percy stepped a little closer to Marcus. "Well you know, I guess I did offer him something, but you already know there's more than two ways out. After all, Dorian did it," Percy said.

"Dorian died, and there's no known life after death in Purgatory, so however he came back is a sheer mystery. I can assure you, he ain't coming back this time. Are you gonna tell me or not?" Marcus asked.

"Tell you what?" Percy asked.

Marcus grabbed him by his torn shirt and pulled him close. "What did you offer Beelzebub?" Marcus asked angrily.

A dagger appeared in Percy's hand just outside of Marcus' view. He held it down low so that Lucifer and Ben wouldn't see it. He looked at Marcus with his good eye and half smiled again. "I offered him you," Percy said. Percy stabbed Marcus in the chest. The tip of the blade emerged out of Marcus' back and he gasped in pain. He let out a brief sigh and stumbled to the floor. Ben ran at Percy who disappeared instantly. Marcus pulled the dagger out of his chest and threw it on the ground beside him. Ben crouched and tried to put his hands over the wound.

Marcus grabbed Ben's jacket and pulled him close. "Don't," he said, "it's a lethal wound. To even try to heal it will kill you."

"Why?" Ben asked.

"Look at your stomach," Marcus said. Ben pulled up his jacket and shirt and looked at his stomach and saw a scar in the exact same spot as where Marcus was stabbed in the alley way.

"What the hell is that?" Ben shrieked.

"That's from the last time you healed me. It's how we heal. We take the punishment. If you try to heal this, you will die," Marcus said.

"He's right Ben, you shouldn't do it," Lucifer said.

"So what," Ben asked, "we're just going to let him die?"

"You have to," Marcus gasped, "I can feel the ichor rising in me."

"What's ichor? Can't we take you to Heaven?"

"No, just... do me a favour," Marcus said.

"What?" Ben asked.

"Get Percy for me."

Marcus burst into ichor. Ben looked down at the puddle on the floor and a tear fell from his eye. He wiped his eye with one finger and stood up and looked at Lucifer with hate in his eyes. "What the hell is ichor?" Ben asked.

Lucifer pointed to the wet cement like substance that Marcus burst into. "That."

"Fucking Percy. First time I met him, and I already want to kill him!" Ben said.

Lucifer looked down at the puddle of ichor in sheer shock. He wasn't sure he had heard correctly, and not only that, Percy had bested Marcus. It was unheard of. Lucifer looked up at Ben. "How the hell did you heal Marcus?" he asked.

"It was when we first realised that Lucas was after me. He got stabbed in the stomach and passed out. I figured angels could heal. Then Marcus told me that only the Seraph can. That's when he figured it out."

They both looked down at the puddle. Anger rose in Ben. All he could think of was Percy. "I'm gonna kill him," he said.

"You'll need help doing that, Ben," Lucifer said.

"Well you're helping me aren't you?" Ben asked.

"Yes, I am."

"I am gonna make him cease to exist," Ben said.

"No, just kill him so that he goes to Purgatory," Lucifer said.

"But why? He killed my friend."

"Let Marcus sort him out. When you're killed and sent to Purgatory, you are powerless. The only way to get your power back is by killing whoever sent you there."

"So we kill Percy here, he goes to Purgatory, and Marcus kills him there, and gets his power back? How do we find Percy?" Ben asked.

"We'll have to ask around," Lucifer said.

CHAPTER IV

"Percy," Beelzebub said, "you have brought me Marcus, so as promised, you are free to go."

Marcus and Percy were standing in a large cave. There was a large staircase of stone in front of them. At the top, was Beelzebub. Marcus was in a daze and trying not to fall over. Percy was in his full human form, as Beelzebub had promised. He turned and looked at Marcus. "Any last words?" he asked.

"Yeah," Marcus said groggily, "I'm gonna rip your fucking head off and shove it down your throat."

"That's quite a statement for an angel in your position," Percy said, "Let's see if you can keep that promise." He laughed and disappeared. Two demons came out of the shadows and grabbed Marcus by an arm each. They dragged him out of the cave and threw him onto the muddy ground, face down. Marcus pushed himself up off the ground and found himself surrounded by decaying bodies of angels and demons. They all stared at him like he was lunch. He wiped the ichor away from his face and stood ready to fight them off. They all lunged at him.

***

Ben and Lucifer were sitting just outside the gates of Heaven looking over the battlefield before them. On the other side of the battlefield they saw the entrance to Purgatory. Ben was looking at it as if he was contemplating storming in there. "Don't even think about it," Lucifer warned.

"Why not?" Ben asked.

"Because you can't just waltz in there and bring him out, that's why not. Even if you were able to get in there, fight your way past all the hungry decaying angels and demons and find him, you won't get him out."

Ben looked down at the ground beneath him. He put his fingers in the dirt of the battlefield and knew that he would be fighting there someday soon. "Why did Percy turn on Marcus anyway?" Ben asked.

"Percy? He wanted the glory of bringing Marcus down. There was no bigger prize to bring down than Marcus. Every demon working on the side of evil wants his blood. Percy just happened to befriend Marcus and then stab him in the back," Lucifer replied.

"You mean the front," Ben added.

"Yes, the front. He was never a coward. He would never go behind your back. If he ever betrayed anyone, he did it in plain view of them, just so they could see it was him. He obviously made a deal with Ugly to bring Marcus to Purgatory."

Ben looked up at Lucifer. "Is he really that ugly?" Ben asked.

"You ever played a computer game called Diablo?" Lucifer asked.

"Yeah, once or twice," Ben said.

"Spitting image of the rat bastard."

"Are you telling me they have computer games in Hell?" Ben laughed.

"You really think I've been in Hell the whole time?" Lucifer asked, "I'll have you know I used to hang out with a lot of famous musicians and actors."

"I know, like Robert Plant," Ben said.

"How did you know that?"

"Oh please, Stairway to Heaven?" Ben said.

"Well, it was probably my best work," Lucifer said, "and I spent some time with computer programmers. I wanted to make sure they got a few things right."

Ben looked back at the entrance to Purgatory. It was a large archway set in stone across the battlefield. The stone wall covered the entire length of the battlefield and curved around it, almost to the white walls of Heaven. Ben looked over to the wall on the left and saw a small dark entrance. "What's that over there?" he asked.

Lucifer looked up at the small cave. "Don't ever go in there!" Lucifer said quickly.

"Why not?" Ben asked.

"Because anybody who has gone in there has never come out."

"So what's in there?"

"Like I said, nobody has ever come out. So how do I know?"

Ben looked back at the entrance to Purgatory. "You want to go see him, don't you?" Lucifer asked.

"We can do that?"

"Well yes, but it's quite dangerous. You don't want to get attacked, or killed. As you know, you're gone for good," Lucifer said.

"I'm willing to risk it," Ben said.

"Okay, let's go. But you won't like it in there."

Lucifer grabbed Ben by the shoulder, and they were instantly both standing on a large rock formation, looking out over the worst site Ben had ever seen. There were bodies lying on the ground everywhere in bits and pieces and most of them were rotted, or rotting. The ground below was like mud and the beings they saw walking around were covered in it. There were giant devils eating flesh off of angels and demons, and angels and demons doing the same. The screams were horrifying. They reminded Ben of the time when Lucifer made his sword and the souls escaped from the steel. The smell though, that was the worst. It was the smell of death, mixed with faeces and blood. Ben began to shake a little as he looked out over the expanse of death. For miles and miles, there was death. He keeled over and began to dry reach. "Easy there, big fella," Lucifer said as he patted Ben on the back.

Ben stood up. "It looks like they've been rolling around in mud and eating each other," he said.

"They pretty much have," Lucifer said, "Come on, open your wings."

They both let their gold wings seep out of their backs and slowly took off up into the air. Everyone below looked up at them as they flew across the dark sky. They looked all over the ground to find anything resembling Marcus as they circled Purgatory, but all they saw was mayhem. Marcus could have been any one of a thousand bodies sinking into the ichor before their ultimate demise. Ben began to worry, hoping and praying that Marcus would be okay. He spotted a familiar figure lying in the mud near a cliff face. "Look, over there," Ben said.

He pointed to the figure lying on the ground, covered in ichor. They flew down and landed in the soft, slushy, muddy liquid. Ben tried to pick his feet up out of it to stop them from getting dirty. He turned around and noticed some demons coming towards them cautiously. Ben pulled out his sword. "Leave them be," Lucifer said, "They won't attack us with our wings open."

"Some of them will try," the figure on the ground said. They turned and looked at Marcus lying there. It looked like he had taken a severe beating, and he was gasping for breaths of air. His hair was wet and almost plastered to his face by the wetness and the ichor.

"What happened to you?" Ben asked.

Marcus looked up at Ben, and then at Lucifer. "Get him out of here," he struggled to say.

"He wanted to see you," Lucifer said, "and so did I. It's going to be quite difficult to find Percy. Any ideas?"

Marcus pushed his hands against the ground to hoist himself up. He was very weak and could barely talk. He eventually sat up and put his back against the cliff face. He tilted his head back and it thudded against the wall. "Go to your sources. They should know where he is. Just get him back here so that I can beat these things."

Lucifer and Ben both nodded together. "We'll do our best," Ben said.

"Get out of here. Now!" Marcus tried to shout. He stood up and leapt in between them and fell on top of a devil that was about to attack them. He grabbed it by the horns and started shaking its head. "Go!" he shouted.

The mighty devil flicked its head and Marcus slammed into the wall. He slowly stood up and rushed at the devil, and launched himself onto its back. He grabbed the horns again as it started running and trying to shake him off. Ben and Lucifer both disappeared and were suddenly both standing back at the gates of Heaven. They looked up at the gates and down at the staircase that lead down to Devils Tower. They began to walk down the staircase and found themselves looking out over the landscape below them. "Why can't we just transport him out?" Ben asked.

"Not possible. It's Purgatory, he's bound there. Plus, he needs to kill Percy to gain his power back."

They both looked at each other. "Well, let's go find him," Ben said.

Marcus violently twisted the head of the devil to the left and he heard its neck snap. It fell to the ground in a heap and he tumbled off of it just before it burst into flames. He stood up and readied himself to fight when he saw Declan standing in front of him. "Marcus, they got you too?" Declan asked.

"Percy," Marcus said.

"Came back to finish the job, huh?" Declan asked.

"Yep. He told Beelzebub he would bring me back, and in doing that he was let out."

"Hopefully, he ends up back here so you can get rid of him."

"I've already got Ben and Lucifer working on it," Marcus said.

"Ah yes, Ben. How is he?"

"He's a Seraph now," Marcus said.

"Already? But that's impossible," Declan said.

"His wings went straight to gold."

"Straight to gold. So he's the…"

Marcus cut him off, "Yes, we believe so". Marcus looked above Declan's head and saw a devil rushing at them. "Look out!" he shouted. Declan turned around and stood next to Marcus, readying himself. Marcus put up a finger to signal Declan to wait. "Wait for it," he said. The devil kept rushing at them fast. It was almost four feet away from them when Marcus reacted. "Now!" he said.

They both ducked as the devil fell on top of them. They both stood up in synchronisation and flipped the devil behind them. It landed on its back. Declan grabbed its legs as Marcus jumped up onto its chest. He raised his boot to kick its face when it put its hands up in fear. "I'm sorry!" it said, "Please don't kill me."

Marcus put his boot back on its chest. "You were about to kill us, why shouldn't we?" Marcus shouted at it.

"I didn't want to do it, but I was told I would be punished if I didn't take you out," it said.

Marcus got down on his knee. "By who?" Marcus asked.

The devil pointed to the direction it came from. Marcus looked up and saw Asmodeus standing in the distance, watching them. He began to walk towards them slowly. As he got closer, he stopped, and half closed his eyes. "Welcome to this nightmare, Marcus," Asmodeus said.

"Aren't you dead yet?" Marcus asked.

"Not quite. You see, I've actually risen up the chain of command here pretty quickly. And now that you're here, I can get rid of you for good."

Asmodeus began running at Marcus and a sword appeared in his hand. Marcus reached up under his jacket and searched for his sword. It wasn't there. Asmodeus held the sword out straight in front of him as a figure emerged from behind him and kicked him just above his backside. Asmodeus stumbled forward and regained his balance, and as he turned around to face his aggressor, a hand came out of nowhere and wrapped itself around his neck. He stopped abruptly in his path and was hoisted into the air. Marcus let his eyes move down the arm and to the body attached to it. It was Azazel. He held Asmodeus high above his head and put his other hand on Asmodeus' shoulder. He pulled down on the shoulder with brute force and ripped Asmodeus' head clean off. He let the body fall to the ground as it burst into flames and threw the head into the distance. It disintegrated like a fireball. Azazel turned and looked at Marcus and smiled. His wings shot up out of his back. They were gold, and no longer mutated. Marcus looked up at the wings and smiled. "Kicked him right in the blurta!" Azazel shrieked.

Marcus looked puzzled. "The what?"

Azazel smirked. "It means bumhole."

"I see..." Marcus replied, "You got your gold wings back! You've been redeemed! I'm really glad to see you, old friend."

"I just wish it was on better terms. Lucifer came to visit and told me what you said to God. Thank you, and thank you for letting me tag along with you, even though I didn't get to see the end. I really enjoyed the journey. You got the sword?" Azazel asked.

"I did, but obviously I'm here. Guess I've gotta wait until I get my power back before I can use it."

Marcus turned around a looked at the devil sitting up on the ground. He walked over to it and held out his hand. "And who might you be?" Marcus asked.

"I'm Timothy," the devil replied.

"Well Tim, there's three of us fighting for the side of good, and we could use you. Are you in?" Marcus asked.

"You're Marcus," Tim said.

"Yes I am. Was that a yes?" Marcus asked again.

"Yes, it would be an honour to join you."

He took Marcus' hand and Marcus helped him up. He towered over the three of them. He would have at least been eight feet tall. They all looked up at him with a certain gratitude that he was on their side. He gave a large reptile-like grin at them, and Marcus looked at Declan. "Okay, well we have a devil and a Seraph with his power back. Let's see who else we can dig up," Marcus said, "provided they're not too far gone."

CHAPTER V

"What are we doing here again?" Lucifer asked Ben.

They were in Ben's lounge room. Ben picked up his staff off the floor. "I had to get my staff. Trust me. If we run into any trouble, you'll thank me," Ben said.

Ben walked through the kitchen and into the hallway. Lucifer walked over to a large picture hanging on the wall. It was a picture of a lighthouse with a large wave washing over it. It looked like a man was standing in the doorway to the lighthouse, about to get washed away. "I never usually trust a man who says trust me," Lucifer said quietly.

Ben came back out into the kitchen with his staff strapped over his shoulder and looked at Lucifer. "Okay, you ready to go?" he asked.

"I've been ready since we got here. I've been waiting for you."

"Okay, where to?" Ben asked.

"I have a friend that might be able to help us out. He's not far from here. Let's go."

They walked out the front door and turned right. Ben ran a little to catch up to Lucifer, and he looked sideways at Ben as he was clutching the strap over his shoulder. "You know you should really learn to hide that thing," he said.

"How am I supposed to hide it? It's as big as I am," Ben asked.

"You remember when you fought Marcus at the house where Dorian lived?" Lucifer asked.

"Yes, what about it?"

"Where did your sword come from?"

Ben looked up and thought for a second, then looked down at the ground to try and jog his memory. He looked up at Lucifer quickly. "It just appeared in my hand! How did I do that?" he asked.

"You did it without thinking, but you believed it would work. So take your staff, hold it in your hand, and convince yourself that it isn't there."

Ben took the strap off his shoulder as he walked and held the staff in his hand and looked at it. "But where will it go?" he asked.

"Wherever you want it to go. Where would it be safest?" Lucifer asked.

"Probably with Michael in Heaven," Ben replied.

"That would probably be the perfect place for it. So imagine that it is no longer in your hand and is safe in the weapons room on the wall." Ben stared at the staff in his hand. It didn't budge an inch, let alone disappear.

"Let me tell you a story," Lucifer said, "There was a class of students waiting to sit an exam. They were all in their seats, checking their watches and tapping pencils on their tables, when the professor walked in. He stood in front of them and welcomed them to their final exam, and then picked up a chair and sat it on top of his desk. He pointed to the chair and told them that the exam was to prove to him that the chair doesn't exist, and he walked out of the room. The whole class failed the exam except for one. That one student only wrote two words. Do you know what those two words were?"

Ben looked up at Lucifer. "What?" he asked.

"What chair?" Lucifer said, "The kid passed the exam for writing those two words. *Two words!* You have to believe it before you can see it. Now, prove to me that your staff isn't in your hand."

Ben looked at his empty hand and then back at Lucifer. "What staff?" he asked.

"That's my boy," Lucifer said.

They continued walking down Ben's street. "Is that story true?" Ben asked.

"Of course it is. Have I lied to you yet? Even when I tried to fight you in Hell, I told you the truth about Marcus letting his guard down, didn't I?" Lucifer asked.

"Yes, you did. So how do I get it back now?" Ben asked.

"Exactly the same way," Lucifer said, "Is your staff in your hand? Of course it is."

Ben looked down at his staff in his hand. "How did you do that?" he asked.

"I didn't. *You* did. You just have to believe, Ben."

Ben looked down at his staff and it disappeared again. "That's really cool," Ben said, "I could become a magician and make so much money."

"It's already been done," Lucifer said, "Houdini did it years ago."

"Wait," Ben stopped and grabbed Lucifer's shoulder, "Houdini was an angel?"

"Of course he was. And then he had to return to Heaven, which is why he died. He just asked for one last trick," Lucifer explained.

"Let me guess, you used to hang out with famous magicians too?" Ben asked.

"No, Marcus was friends with Houdini, not me. Michael told Marcus to send him back."

They continued walking. "Why did Michael ask Marcus to send him back? Couldn't he have just asked himself?" Ben asked.

"It's not just demons that fear Marcus you know, it's angels too. When he eventually grew up, he was much respected. I guess he never saw that. He has become just like his father."

"You mean *your* father," Ben said.

"Yes, mine too," Lucifer said, "I was never much of a warrior; more of a scholar. I preferred to read instead of fight. You see, when I was a Cherub, my wings were red. Blue is a warrior, and red is a scholar. So, who do you think our old daddy paid more attention to? Of course, when I became a Seraph, I learnt to fight, and I became more involved in what defending Heaven was all about. And then, I saw freedom. Humans walking the Earth, with every right to anything they want. Except to taste the fruit of a certain tree. No, that was forbidden. He taught them to obey rules, and I taught them to break them. Breaking rules is what fighting is all about.

Marcus breaks rules all the time, you know that. Why shouldn't humans have the right to learn that sometimes it's okay to break the rules? Where would the world be today if they hadn't learned to break the rules?"

"It would probably be a sanctuary of peace," Ben said.

"It would be far less advanced. How many people throw away the rule book these days and act on their own intuition to better a situation?"

"Lots of people do. Any authority figure will tell you that it's okay to break the rules every now and then, if it's the right thing to do."

"That's what I was trying to teach!" Lucifer shrieked.

"But they disobeyed God," Ben said.

"But they learnt shame. They learnt redemption. If I left a pizza for you, but said 'Don't eat it', what would you do?"

"I'd probably wait until you weren't looking and then have a piece," Ben said.

"Exactly," Lucifer said, "And you would do that because that's exactly what Adam and Eve did. If he didn't want them to have the fruit, then why did he put the tree there in the first place? To test them, that's why. He gave them free will, and in testing their free will, I was punished. I guess he never realised I was doing it for him and for mankind. I was exiled, and anyone who defended me was kicked out with me. But I will forever be remembered as the snake that tried to lure humankind into a world of evil. The word was written by the hand of a man who wasn't even there to witness the events. Chinese whispers; a story that somebody once told."

"You have been in Hell far too long," Ben said.

"You don't have to tell *me* that. Anyway, all is forgiven now. God knows that I wasn't trying to lure them to evil. You people have had enough of that with Ugly trying to sway your thoughts, and tempt your minds," Lucifer said.

They kept walking in silence, and turned left at the end of the street, walking past a few neon signs advertising nudity. They walked beneath one of the neon signs and through a doorway into a strip club. There was a man standing just inside the door, looking at the two of them. He shook hands with Lucifer. "He's in the back," the man said, as he looked at Ben, "Who is this?"

"He's my friend. Let him in," Lucifer said.

Ben fought off a boyish smile. Lucifer had just called him his friend. Ben walked past the man and followed Lucifer into the room. The bar was on their right and there was a stage on their left, to the back of the room with a girl dancing in white lingerie in front of a pole. There were tables set up all around the room with a few middle aged men sitting down and watching the girl on the stage. Lucifer walked to a door in the back and walked through it, and Ben followed him. Through the door was a small, dimly lit hallway with another door at the end. The music from the other room was still present, but a little muffled. They walked to the door at the end of the hallway and Lucifer knocked on it. The door opened and they saw a man standing there looking at them with a white t-shirt and long blonde hair. He was very well built with a large chest, and it looked like his muscles were about to pop out of his t-shirt. "Lucifer!" the man said.

He put his hand on Lucifer's shoulder and put his other arm around Lucifer's back. He thumped on Lucifer's shoulder blade with a closed fist and stepped away quickly, almost as if hugging wasn't something he did all that often. "Please, come in," he said, "Who's your friend?"

He turned around and walked into the small room and sat down on a leather couch. There was a leather couch sitting opposite, which Ben and Lucifer sat down in. "This is Ben," Lucifer said, "Marcus' most recent prodigy."

"So you're one of Marcus' boys?" the man asked.

"Not just one of them. The best," Lucifer added as he turned to Ben, "This is Gabriel."

"Gabriel? As in *the* Gabriel?" Ben asked.

"The one and only," Gabriel said.

"You're one of the most feared angels," Ben said.

"Was. Marcus is the big cheese now," Gabriel said.

"So I've heard," Ben said.

"Welcome to my humble abode. Any friend of these guys is a friend of mine," Gabriel looked at Lucifer, "Where is Marcus, anyway?"

"That's kind of why we're here," Lucifer said.

Gabriel looked at Lucifer in shock. "Percy is back, isn't he?" he asked.

"Oh yeah," Lucifer said, "he's back alright. Now, do you know where Marcus is?"

"Well, if Percy is back, then he gave Marcus to Beelzebub, which means Marcus is dead."

"In a manner of speaking," Lucifer said, "You haven't seen Percy?"

"Why would I see Percy?" Gabriel asked.

"We figure he might try to contact some of the boys. Have you heard what's been going on?" Lucifer asked.

"I heard that Marcus got his sword back, and that you're allowed back into Heaven, finally. Other than that, I haven't heard much else."

"Ben, wings," Lucifer said.

Ben's gold wings rose up out of his back. Gabriel looked up at them and smiled. "Marcus must have trained you well," Gabriel said.

"Ben was a human," Lucifer said, "and his wings went straight to gold."

Gabriel's jaw dropped. He looked at Ben's wings and then down at his face. "But that means he's the…"

"Yep. Sure does."

Gabriel smiled. "It's all true then. All of it. Marcus got his sword back, and now we have the human angel. This is almost surreal," Gabriel said.

"And I'm guessing the angel has fallen, since Marcus is in Purgatory," Lucifer said, "The second paragraph of the Revelation."

"Can somebody please enlighten me?" Ben asked, "I've never read this thing, and I have no idea what it says."

"That's the other reason I brought you here," Lucifer said, "Gabriel, can we see it please?"

Gabriel nodded. He stood up and walked over to a painting on the wall. It was a painting of the last supper, with Jesus sitting in the middle of all of his apostles. Ben stuck his neck out and studied it, as if stretching his neck would get him closer to the painting. Gabriel grabbed the side of the painting and swung it open like a door. There was a safe in the wall behind it with a dial on the front. Gabriel turned the dial three times and opened the safe. He pulled out an old looking leather bound scroll, with a red ribbon wrapped around it. He closed the safe again, and put the painting back in its place. He walked back to the couch and sat down and handed the scroll to Ben, who took it carefully and pulled on the bow of the red ribbon. The scroll slightly unraveled as the ribbon came loose. Ben opened the scroll up with one hand at the top, and one at the bottom. He read the Revelation.

Ben looked up at Gabriel with a tear in his eye, as he had realised he was a part of it. He turned to look at Lucifer for confirmation. "Yes, it's the Revelation, Ben," Lucifer said.

Ben rolled up the scroll. "Gabriel is the Guardian," Lucifer said, "It was given to him to be protected from anyone, or anything."

"So why is it on Earth?" Ben asked.

"Because Gabriel is on Earth. The scroll is safest with the Guardian, wherever he chooses to live."

"The one thing that I don't get is that the current events are backwards. It says in the third paragraph after the angel has fallen and then risen, an angel will be born of human blood. From what I can see, the identity of the human angel has been discovered, and the angel has fallen, but not yet risen," Gabriel said.

"You have a point there," Lucifer said, "Could there be more to it?"

"That's the entire Revelation," Gabriel said, "I watched God write it myself."

Ben looked at the scroll in his hand. "God wrote this?" he asked.

"Who else would have?" Gabriel asked, "But he was always cryptic; always spoke in riddles. There could be more between the lines."

Ben handed the scroll back to Gabriel who stood up and walked back over to the painting. He pulled the painting aside and opened the safe again, placing the scroll carefully inside. He closed the safe and put the painting back into place. "Could there be another angel that has fallen and risen?" Ben asked.

"When you think about it, Lucifer, you were apparently the fallen angel. And now you have been granted access back into Heaven. That could be a meaning of it. Was it only after you were allowed back into Heaven that you realised that Ben is the human angel?" Gabriel asked.

"Well, yes actually," Lucifer said.

"That could be it, then. So what do we do about Marcus? There are only two ways out of there, and unless you find Percy so that Marcus can get his power back, I don't see him offering any deals to Dickless," Gabriel said, "I mean Beelzebub. Even though..."

Gabriel stopped in thought for a moment. He had almost said too much. He was one of the only ones that knew that Marcus had escaped from Purgatory before. He sat back, pretending he wasn't about to say something. Ben looked down at the ground, collecting his thoughts. Lucifer saw the cogs turning in his head. "What are you thinking?" he asked.

Ben looked up at Lucifer. "You said earlier that you figured Percy might try to contact some of the boys. Who are the boys?" Ben asked.

Gabriel sat forward and looked at Ben. "Have you ever heard of the Angels of War?" he asked.

"No, I haven't," Ben said.

"The Angels of War consisted of six members; Marcus, Declan, Caius, Zennah, Percy and me. We were a fierce group. Put the six of us into battle, and pray for anyone who opposed us. We were an elite force, put together by the Archangel Michael himself. Percy was only involved because he was Marcus' wing man, and he was very good. Michael used to compliment Marcus' teaching."

"Declan is also in Purgatory," Lucifer said, "Baal killed him a few days ago."

"I'm very sad to hear that," Gabriel said, "It looks like I'm the only one left."

"What do you mean?" Ben asked.

"Caius and Zennah dropped off the radar years ago. Haven't seen them for a long time."

"What were they doing?" Lucifer asked.

"Well, I heard Declan got himself into law enforcement, and Caius did something similar. As for Zennah, she became some sort of mercenary, but her and the Valkyrie would no doubt come and help, if they were asked. I don't know where you'll find her now. If Declan is dead, then I fear that those two may have ended up with the same fate. After all, Baal wasn't exactly our best friend," Gabriel explained.

"Marcus killed Baal," Lucifer said.

"So, he ended up back at home. What a travesty for him," Gabriel said.

"No, Marcus killed him in Purgatory," Lucifer said.

Gabriel raised his eyebrows and stared at Lucifer. "Are you telling me that Baal is gone for good?" he asked.

"He ain't coming back," Lucifer said.

"Well that's a relief," Gabriel said, "I was hoping I wouldn't have to see him again. If Caius and Zennah have ended up in Purgatory, I can guarantee you Marcus will find them."

"I don't know if Caius will want to see Marcus again," Lucifer said.

"Who are Caius and Zennah? I've never heard you mention them before," Ben asked.

Lucifer looked at Ben with a smile. "Caius is cupid," Lucifer said.

Ben opened his eyes wide. "You mean there really *is* a cupid?" he asked.

Both Gabriel and Lucifer laughed. "Well, sort of. His weapon of choice was a bow. At one point, he was friends with a human, who was in love with a certain woman. He couldn't quite capture her attention, until he was injured. Caius knew it was the only way. He helped him by shooting an arrow into his chest, and the woman he was in love with came to his side and fell in love with him. Of course, that's the only thing he did that humans actually witnessed. If they witnessed anything else, they would have called him the devil. He was a loose cannon, and he had a temper to match," Lucifer explained.

"Let's not forget Zennah. She should be ruling Hell alongside you," Gabriel said.

"That bad, huh?" Ben asked.

"She would always have a dagger in each hand. And believe me, we were always thankful that she was on our side," Gabriel said.

"I hope that Percy isn't as persuasive as he used to be. If he finds her, she might change her tune," Lucifer said.

"I don't know. She always adored Marcus, and Percy betrayed him. She'd want his blood just like the rest of us," Gabriel said.

"So, you don't know where the other two are?" Lucifer asked.

"Like I said, I haven't seen them in years. If you find them, tell them to drop me a line," Gabriel said, "And if we're heading for the Great War, you can count me in. You know where to find me."

"Thank you, Gabriel. I'm sure we'll be seeing you very soon," Lucifer said.

"I hope so," Gabriel said, "Good to see you again Lucifer. And Ben, it was a pleasure to meet you. Best of luck to you, my brother."

"Thank you," Ben said, as he shook Gabriel's hand.

They walked out of the room and through the hallway into the bar. After looking around at the faces in the room, they walked out of the exit and Lucifer nodded to the man in the doorway as they walked past him into the cold night air. Lucifer looked up at the stars. "So what do we do now?" Ben asked.

Lucifer turned and looked at him. "I guess we have to go talk to Marcus," Lucifer said.

Chapter VI

Marcus was sitting on a rock. playing with the ring on his thumb, looking at it very closely and tracing his thumb across the tribal etchings on it. He pulled his right jacket sleeve back and looked at the identical etchings on the cuff around his wrist, remembering that Arus had given him the ring all those years ago. The ring was part of the set. He recalled putting on the identical ring in the cave in Chislehurst and looking at them next to each other. He had worn the ring on his thumb for so long, he had almost forgotten its significance. Marcus kept twirling it around his thumb as it loosened, and fell to the ground. He quickly picked it up as Declan snorted a small laugh. "Didn't anybody ever tell you? You keep playing with it, it'll fall off!"

Marcus gave Declan a stunned look, then laughed. Declan was sitting down on Marcus' left, and Azazel was standing off to his right. Tim was standing in front of them, keeping a lookout over the crowd of deformed and decayed beings. There were a few other angels and demons sitting around them. Marcus saw Ben and Lucifer coming towards him, and stood up instantly. "What are you doing here? Any luck?" he asked.

Lucifer shook his head. "No luck I'm afraid," Lucifer said, "We went to see Gabriel, and he hasn't seen him."

"I didn't think he'd try to contact the old crew," Marcus said, "they want to kill him as much as I do. Did Ben see it?"

"Yes, I read it," Ben said.

"Good," Marcus said, "Now you have a better understanding?"

"Yes," Ben said, "and no."

"It's okay, it'll all become clear soon enough. He, uh, didn't say anything else, did he?"

Ben raised his eyebrows. "Like what?"

Marcus shook his head. "Never mind."

Declan stood up and joined in the conversation. "How is Gabe?" he asked, "Haven't seen him in years."

"Declan!" Lucifer said, "Good to see you again. He's not too bad, but apparently he hasn't seen the other two in years either. Have you?"

Declan shook his head. "I saw Caius once," he said, "He's a police officer now, somewhere. As for Zennah, haven't heard a thing."
"She's in England," Marcus said.

Declan, Lucifer and Ben all looked at Marcus. "How do you know that?" Lucifer asked.

They all stared at him with intrigue. They all knew he and Zennah were close. All except Ben. "We catch up every now and then. Quit staring at me," Marcus said.

"How do we find Percy?" Ben asked.

Marcus looked at him with a degree of respect. He liked the angel that Ben was becoming. Straight to the point. "Nimrod," Marcus said.

"Nimrod?" Lucifer asked, "Where have I heard that before?"

"He's a hunter, an archangel, and he hunts demons," Marcus said.

Ben looked at Marcus with a puzzled look on his face. "Read your bible!" Marcus said.

"Where do we find Nimrod?" Lucifer asked.

"Huntington," Marcus said, "He's onto something big there. Check out the local clubs. There was an old bar on the east side of town with a blue stone wall, and I usually found him there."

"Marcus, I grew up there, remember?" Ben asked.

"Oh yeah, that's right, I forgot. Your parents live there. How are they?" Marcus asked.

"Last time I saw them was with you," Ben said.

"Always liked your parents. Especially your dad, he's funny as hell," Marcus said.

"Do you know this bar?" Lucifer asked, "With the blue stone wall?"

"Yeah," Ben said, "I know where it is."

"Alright then," Lucifer said, "Let's go find Nimrod."

Ben put his hand on Lucifer's shoulder, and Lucifer put his hand on top of Ben's. "Are you confident enough in your transporting to be able to bring me with you?" Lucifer asked.

"Yeah, I just gotta believe," Ben said.

Marcus smiled. "I'm proud of you, Ben," Marcus said.

"Thanks," Ben said.

Ben and Lucifer found themselves standing in a small alleyway in broad daylight. Ben walked down to the end of the alley into a small street with cars parked down one side. He looked left and right, and beckoned Lucifer over. Lucifer came out of the alley and followed Ben left as they walked down the street. They walked over the road and past a blue stone wall, and then up to the entrance to a Scottish themed bar. They walked up the three steps and in through the glass doors to the bar. It was a long room from side to side. On their right at the far end was a small red stage against a blue stone wall, and the high roof was all glass. There was a long bar in front of them that almost ran from one end of the room to the other. The bar curved around towards the back wall in an 'L' shape. There was a man sitting at the end of the bar with a drink in front of him. He had a shaved head and the hair of his chin hung down to his neck like a spear head. There was a man behind the bar polishing wine glasses and hanging them in racks above the bar. "Hi guys, what can I get for ya?" the bartender asked.

Ben walked up to the bar and looked at the large wall of spirits behind the man. He spotted a box of Johnnie Walker Blue up on the top shelf, and looked to his left towards the end of the bar. There was an opening for the staff to get through, and then the bar became a kitchen. He noticed an automatic teller machine at the end of the room next to an old fashioned red phone booth. "I remember you," the bartender said, "You were in here a few years ago talking to me about martial arts."

"Yeah, that's right," Ben said.

Ben put a fifty dollar note on the bar. "I'll have a Johnnie Blue, thanks.'

The bartender raised his eyebrows and half smiled. He looked up at Lucifer, and Lucifer shrugged. "I guess I'll have the same."

"Excellent choice," the bartender said. He was a tall man, and it wasn't much of a stretch for him to reach up to the top shelf to grab the box. He pulled it down and carefully removed the bottle from the box, and popped the cork lid off, sitting the bottle on the bench below the wall of spirits. He reached under the bar and came up with two glasses. "You're not going to ask for ice, are you?" he asked.

"No, no ice thanks," Ben said.

"Good," the bartender said, "Ice waters it down too much. Ruins it."

He poured the two glasses and sat them on the bar next to each other. He picked the fifty dollar bill up off the bar and rung it up in the cash register, but didn't give any change. "Fifty bucks for two of these?" Lucifer asked.

The bartender nodded. "Twenty five bucks a shot."

Lucifer closed his eyes and shook his head. "This had better be the best Johnnie Blue I've ever tasted." He took a small sip and let it settle in his mouth. He looked up and savoured the taste, and then looked back at the bartender. "Lucky," he said.

They pulled up two stools and sat at the bar. "Consider yourself lucky," the bartender said, "They charge fifty bucks in the city. They sell six shots and the bottle is practically paid for. So how long are you boys in town?"

"We're leaving tonight, actually. We're here looking for somebody," Ben said.

"In Huntington? Or in this pub?"

"In this pub," Ben said, "He usually hangs out here. Some people call him Nimrod."

The bartender glanced left at the man sitting at the end of the bar. He looked back at Ben and Lucifer. "Don't know of any regulars with that name, sorry."

Ben glanced at the man sitting at the end of the bar and looked back at the bartender. "I know a cover up when I see one. Thank you." He picked up his drink, walked to the end of the bar and sat down next to the man with the shaved head and the beard. "I'm Ben," he said, "Marcus sent me here to find you."

The man was staring at his drink on the bar. He moved his head and looked at Ben's drink as if he were looking at Ben. "You are interfering with my work. And if I'm found out, I will hunt you down and kill you," Nimrod said.

"You are an Archangel," Ben said, "I am a Seraph. I highly doubt you will hunt me down and kill me. Over there, that's Lucifer, Marcus' brother. There are a few more things at stake right now than your cover being blown."

The bartender walked down the bar towards Ben and Nimrod. "I think you should leave, okay? I don't like my customers being bothered."

Nimrod put his hand up. "It's okay. They're friends, not foes." The bartender walked back to the wine glasses and began polishing again. "Why would Marcus send you two to find me?" Nimrod asked.

"Because Marcus is dead," Ben explained, "We need you to locate the demon that killed him so that we can send him back to Purgatory for Marcus to gain his power back."

Nimrod smiled. "Marcus is in Purgatory? I highly doubt that. So who killed him?"

Ben stared at Nimrod for a long second. "Take a wild guess."

Nimrod looked up at the spirits on the wall for a second and opened his eyes wide. "It was Percy, wasn't it?"

"The one and only," Ben said.

Lucifer walked over to join them. "And you're Lucifer. It's a pleasure. I've never actually had the chance to meet you," Nimrod said as he shook Lucifer's hand.

"I don't think many angels in your position have had the chance. So why are you hiding out here?" Lucifer asked.

"I'm not hiding. There's some nasty stuff going on in this town, and I'm trying to find the source. There has been a lot of violence, and it doesn't look like it was caused by humans," Nimrod said.

"You should look at the nightclub owners," Ben said.

"No," Nimrod said, "They'd lose too much business by their venues gaining a bad reputation. It's someone that is trying to get rid of certain people. I think Percy is now higher on my agenda, though."

"So you'll help us?" Ben asked.

"Well, I have to. Marcus sent you," Nimrod said, "Where was Percy last seen?"

"In New York," Ben said, "That was where he killed Marcus."

"No doubt he would have gone back to Purgatory to claim his freedom. And then I figure he would go back to familiar territory. Demons always prefer familiarity. Since the Angels of War used to reside in New York, I guess he'll start there, so that's where we'll start." Nimrod stood up and picked up his jacket off the bar. He put it around his broad shoulders and threaded his arms through the sleeves. Ben and Lucifer finished their drinks and left the glasses on the bar. They waved to the bartender on their way out through the glass doors, and turned left, walking past the blue stone wall back towards the alley. "So, where are we meeting?" Nimrod asked.

"Murphy's," Ben replied, "Do you know where it is?"

"Yes, Marcus and I have been there before."

"Meet us there. My house isn't too far."

Nimrod disappeared. Lucifer and Ben found themselves standing in the alleyway behind Murphy's where Ben was attacked by Lucas and the demons. He remembered the small one that looked like a little baby demon and slightly shuddered. They walked around the front and into the front door of Murphy's under the neon sign. They sat at the bar and nodded to Mike. "Hey guys, welcome back. Usual?" Mike asked.

"I'll have the usual. What do you want?" Ben asked Lucifer.

"I'll have a beer, thanks."

Mike poured a scotch and coke for Ben and sat it in front of him, then grabbed a glass mug and poured a beer for Lucifer. He sat the beer in front of Lucifer. "On the tab?" he asked.

"Yep, thanks," Ben said.

They sipped their drinks and waited for Nimrod. "Do you think he'll actually show up?" Ben asked.

"Of course I will. As I said, Marcus sent you, so I have to," Nimrod said from just behind them.

They turned and looked at him. "So what are you drinking?"
Ben asked.

"Same as you, by the look of things," he answered.

Nimrod nodded to the bartender. "Scotch and coke, tall glass,
no ice. Thanks," Nimrod said.

"On my tab please, Mike," Ben said.

"No problems," Mike replied. He poured the drink and
handed it to Nimrod, and then walked away to write up the
tab.

Nimrod took a sip of his drink. "By the way, I've already
located Percy," Nimrod said.

Ben and Lucifer both sat up straight and stared at Nimrod.
"What? Where?" Lucifer asked.

Nimrod pointed with his head to the pool table. Ben and
Lucifer both looked towards the pool table and saw Percy
standing there, watching a game of pool being played. He
looked completely normal, with a full human figure. His
longish brown hair fell down both sides of his face. Ben stood
up instantly and his sword appeared in his hand. "Ben, no.
We're in public," Lucifer said.

Ben looked down at the sword and it disappeared. He looked
back up at the pool table and saw Percy staring right at him.
Percy stepped around the pool table and stared at the three of

them. He calmly walked past them and made his way over to the toilet door and walked in. Ben followed him. When he got into the bathroom he saw that Percy wasn't there. Percy had disappeared. Ben walked back out of the toilets and up to Lucifer and Nimrod. "He's gone," he said, "You sure he isn't a coward?"

"Positive," Lucifer said, "He knows that we're after him, and I can guarantee he doesn't want to go back to Purgatory any time soon, especially with Marcus there. Naturally, he will avoid us."

"Do you think he knows who I am?" Ben asked.

"I think he has an idea," Lucifer said.

"I think he's scared of me," Ben said.

"Don't get too cocky. Don't forget, he brought Marcus down."

"That was a cheap shot. He shouldn't even get the credit for that," Ben said.

"That's his nature. He'll take any chance he can get."

Ben looked at Nimrod. "Can you find him again?" he asked.

"Without a doubt. Let's go back to your place," Nimrod said.

They finished their drinks and walked out the front door, and turned left, walking east towards Ben's street. "I still think he'll try to contact the old crew," Lucifer said.

"You heard what Gabriel said. They all want a piece of him," Ben said.

"Maybe not Caius," Lucifer said.

"Why not?" Ben asked.

"Because Caius liked Zennah, and Zennah liked Marcus. They had a falling out over it."

"So there's love in Heaven too," Ben said.

"There's love everywhere," Lucifer said.

"So there's no chance that the Angels of War will reunite?"

"Well for one, they won't reunite with Percy. In my eyes, there is no more Angels of War."

They turned left into Ben's street and walked up to his front door. He opened the door and they stepped inside. Ben sat down on the couch and Lucifer walked over to the picture of the lighthouse on the wall again. Nimrod sat down on the couch next to Ben and held his hands together. He put his head on his hands and closed his eyes. Ben looked at him. "Are you okay?" he asked.

"Be quiet," Lucifer said, "he's working."

Nimrod's light brown wings began to rise out of his back. He began rocking back and forth. His eyes opened. "He's close by," Nimrod said.

"Where?" Ben asked.

"Two streets over to the east. Demon household."

"Well let's go," Ben said, jumping up and walking quickly towards the door. The other two followed him. He ran to the end of the street, turned left and began to jog. They made it to the second street over and Nimrod grabbed Ben by the shoulder and put his finger to his lips to tell Ben to be quiet. They walked quietly down the street and Nimrod stopped outside a house with the porch light on and muffled music coming from inside. Ben walked quietly down the driveway and up to one of the windows with the light on. He peered inside and saw three men sitting around the room, and Percy standing over by the far wall. He crouched and crawled under the window and motioned with his arm for the other two to join him. He made it to the front door and stood up. The other two crept under the window and joined Ben at the door. Ben tried to picture the inside of the house in his head. He imagined a hallway running straight, and the room he saw Percy in would be the first door to the right.

Ben's sword appeared in his hand and he kicked the door open. It burst out of the lock and swung away from him to the left. He rushed inside and saw a small hallway with two doors on the right, one on the left, and one at the end. He quickly turned into the first door on the right. Percy was still standing against the wall, but was looking straight at Ben. The three sitting on the couch had all stood up and were ready to fight. There was a door to the back of the room, right next to where Percy was standing. Percy rushed out through the door and the three men all jumped at Ben. Then, they saw Lucifer and Nimrod standing in the doorway behind Ben and stopped and backed off a little. Ben stepped into the room and looked towards the doorway where Percy had run out. Lucifer and Nimrod walked around Ben and moved towards the three men in the room. Ben ran through the door in the back of the room. He came into a kitchen. At the back of the kitchen was the back door, and it was half open. He threw it all the way open and stepped out into the night air. He looked all around him, but couldn't see Percy anywhere. He turned to walk back into the house and was hit by a baseball bat. He fell to the floor. Ben jumped up quickly and saw Percy standing there with a baseball bat in his hand. "Who the hell do you think you are?" Percy asked, "Do you have any idea what you're up against?"

Ben wiped his face and glared at Percy. "I know exactly what I'm up against. A pitiful, cowardly demon."

"Oh, I'm a coward? I'm sure you've been hanging around with Marcus long enough for him to tell you that I'm no coward."

"He mentioned it. Quite frankly, I don't see it," Ben said.

"Who are you anyway?" Percy asked.

"I'm the human angel," Ben said.

"You? Yes, nice one. I'll believe that when I see it," Percy said.

Ben let his gold wings seep out of his back and moved quickly towards Percy. Lucifer and Nimrod came in through the door at the front of the kitchen. "It's true, Percy. Ben is the human angel. His wings went straight to gold. And you'll never guess who his teacher was," Lucifer said.

"Oh, so you're Ben," Percy said, "Why, everyone has been talking about you."

"What are you talking about?" Ben asked.

"Well, you're Marcus' little project. You got your wings and then all of a sudden you become a Seraph. Lucky you, I guess. But you're not what everyone thinks you are. Just look at you."

Ben's sword disappeared. Within a second, his bow staff appeared in his hand. He lunged at Percy and fell to the floor, and when he looked up and saw that Percy was gone. "Where did he go?" Ben asked.

"He just disappeared," Nimrod said.

"Ah!" Ben growled, "I told you, he's a fucking coward! We need him to stay still!"

"You know, Marcus might know his weakness," Nimrod said.

"Hey, that's a great idea," Lucifer said, "Let's go see him." The three of them disappeared.

CHAPTER VII

"What do you plan to do once you kill Percy?" Declan asked Marcus.

"What do you think?" Marcus replied.

"I think you should consider the alternative."

"I'll never make a deal. Besides, what could I possibly give Beelzebub that he would prefer, over me?"

"His own life. You could turn it into a threat. He lets you go, or you kill him. Even he is afraid of you."

"And if he doesn't accept, I'll have to go back to plan A," Marcus said.

At that moment, Ben, Lucifer and Nimrod came walking up to Marcus. He was sitting on the same rock next to Declan, with a slightly larger army of angels and demons around him. "Well, it didn't take you long to climb the ladder," Lucifer said.

"How's the search going?" Marcus asked.

"We've seen him a few times, but he keeps disappearing before we get the chance to take him down. We need to know some of his secrets," Ben said.

"What, you mean his weaknesses?" Marcus asked.

"Yep. We need to stop him from transporting."

A smile formed on Marcus' face. He had a glimpse of hope in his eyes. "He's afraid of heights."

"Heights?" Ben asked, "He's a demon. Doesn't he have wings?"

"No, he has one wing," Marcus said, "I take full credit for that one." Marcus and Declan bumped fists together and chuckled.

"So how can we exploit that?" Lucifer asked.

"He can't transport when he's afraid. Surprise him and take him to Devils Tower. He never liked it up there, even when he had both of his wings. I used to make him wait there when I went into Heaven," Marcus said.

"How long ago was this? How long were you friends?"

"Well, I was allowed into Heaven, so longer than seven hundred years ago, and he betrayed me only twenty years ago."

"That's a long time," Ben said.

"Yep, it kinda makes me wonder how he could have ever done what he did."

"I'm gonna fucking kill him!" Ben said.

"Easy boy," Marcus said, "You're getting very angry these days."

"The piece of shit killed my best friend. Wouldn't you be angry?" Ben asked.

"I am angry," Marcus said, "I am your best friend, so how do you think I feel?"

Ben shrugged.

"Just send him here soon," Marcus said, "I'm getting sick of being grounded."

"Consider it done." Ben, Lucifer and Nimrod all disappeared.

"He's becoming very feisty!" Marcus said, "I love it!"

"He's quickly becoming more and more like you," Declan said.

"What do you expect? I taught him everything he knows. I just had no idea he had such a thirst for vengeance."

"So do you," Declan replied.

"Yes, I do," Marcus replied.

***

Lucifer and Nimrod were sitting on Ben's couch. Nimrod was rocking back and forth like he had before, with his head resting on his hands. Ben walked out of his hallway and through the kitchen into the lounge room, carrying a bunch of black clothes in his hands. He was dressed all in black with a hooded sweatshirt on top. He threw the black clothes on the kitchen bench and turned around to wait for Nimrod to come out of his trance. Nimrod opened his eyes. "He's at a house that's been burned to the ground. It's in New York, but not anywhere nearby," he said.

"Burned to the ground?" Lucifer asked, "Not Sam's house?"

"Samael?" Nimrod asked, "Yes, in fact it looks a lot like his neighbourhood. When did the house burn down?"

"A few days ago, thanks to Marcus," Lucifer said.

"Interesting. The plot thickens. He's rummaging through the rubble. As Marcus said, we need to surprise him," Nimrod said.

"That's what the black clothes are for," Ben said, looking at the clothes on the bench, "They should fit you guys." Lucifer and Nimrod stood up and walked over to the clothes on the bench. They began sorting through them to see what would fit them. They each had their handfuls and looked at Ben. "Down the hallway. Bathroom is at the end, and my room is the first door on the right. Take your pick," Ben said.

Lucifer and Nimrod walked through the kitchen and into the hallway, while Ben walked over to the couch and sat down. He reached to the table beside the couch and opened a draw underneath the tabletop. He pulled out some fingerless gloves and slid them onto his hands, then stood up and pulled his hood over his head. Lucifer walked out of the hallway in the clothes that he took from the bench. He sat down on the couch and waited for Nimrod, who came out of the hallway seconds later. The long sleeved t-shirt he was wearing was rather tight for his broad shoulders. He looked up at Ben. "I'd better not be wearing this for very long," he said, "It's a bit tight."

"It's okay, it won't take long," Ben said, "Let's go. Alleyway behind Sam's place." Ben disappeared.

"He's feisty," Nimrod said.

"He's beginning to take after Marcus, in many ways," Lucifer said, "See you at Sam's."

They both found themselves in the alleyway behind Sam's place, and saw a black figure peering over the fence. He jumped down and turned around to see them. "He's still there," Ben whispered.

Ben grabbed the top of the fence with both of his hands and hoisted himself over in one quick movement, and his feet landed softly on the grass on the other side. Lucifer was next over the fence. He landed right next to Ben. Nimrod peered over the fence. "You guys go. I'll stay here," he said.

Ben and Lucifer tiptoed forward towards Percy who was rummaging through some burnt out junk on the ground. They silently rushed up to him and grabbed an arm each from behind. "Guess who?" Ben asked.

Percy shook himself violently to try to escape. The three of them were instantly standing on top of Devils Tower. They had Percy right at the edge looking down at the ground below. He let out a small yelp and staggered backwards. They let go of his arms. Ben removed his hood and glared at Percy with such a flame in his eyes. Percy looked at the two of them and began to laugh. "What's so funny?" Ben asked.

Percy held both of his arms out as both of his wings grew out of his back. One was unscathed, whereas the other looked like it used to belong to another demon, and had been roughly sewn on. Percy began floating up above the tower. The stairway that led up to Heaven was just behind him. Ben looked up at Percy's wings and then down at his sword, which was now in his hand. *Think like Marcus*, he thought. He looked back up at Percy's good wing and flung the sword at it. The sword spun through the air, and in its last arc before it hit, it rotated to the right angle and sliced Percy's good wing off. He fell down and landed at the foot of the staircase, and looked up at Ben in fear. Ben still had anger in his eyes. His staff appeared in his hand and he walked up to Percy and began hitting him in the face with one end of it. He kept on hitting him until he was puffed out. Ben stood up and his staff disappeared. He got down on one knee and brought his hands up to his face and closed his eyes. Percy stood up in a daze and looked down at Ben. "What are you doing?" he asked, "praying?"

Ben stood up and walked right up to Percy. He pulled his right shoulder back, and put his left palm over his right fist. He thrust both hands forward and pierced them straight through Percy's stomach. Percy let out a scream of pain. Ben began to move his hands away from each other, gradually splitting Percy in two from the stomach up and down. He wrenched his hands apart as far as they would go, and Percy landed in two pieces on the top of Devils Tower before he burst into ichor. Ben was puffing and panting, when Lucifer came over to him with caution. He put his hand on Ben's shoulder. "You didn't have to torture him," Lucifer said.

"Yes I did. That's the move that Marcus never taught him," Ben said.

"You and Marcus, you're so violent!" Lucifer said.

They walked up the steps to Heaven and up to the gates. Lucifer grabbed Ben's shoulder again. "You did really well back there. You're becoming a fine angel. I wish Marcus could have seen that," Lucifer said.

"Thanks," Ben said, as he smiled.

Lucifer saw Ben in a new light. He had technically lost his brother, but he had gained a very valuable new friend. He knew that Ben was by far the best that Marcus had ever trained, and he was a human. Lucifer smiled back at Ben and tapped his palm on his shoulder as a well done gesture. They sat down outside the gates of Heaven and looked over the battlefield towards the gates of Purgatory.

***

Percy landed in the mud like liquid on the ground. He looked up and saw decaying bodies walking towards him. He quickly stood up and turned a full circle, and saw them coming from every direction. He had been in this situation before, and he knew what they were walking towards him for. *Fresh meat,* he thought as he stared at all of them advancing on him. Then suddenly, they stopped. He turned around to see them all standing in a large circle around him, just staring at him. He noticed that a gap was forming in the circle. The decaying bodies were making way for someone, or something. Marcus emerged from the gap and started walking towards Percy. "This one's mine," he said.

Marcus walked right up to Percy and stood with his nose just an inch away from his. His nostrils flared and his eyes showed nothing but pure hatred for him. Percy looked away from Marcus' intimidating stare. The first rule of staring; the first one to look away, loses. Percy looked back up at Marcus and realised he had just lost. He swung his right fist at Marcus' face, and it was stopped instantly by something soft, but firm. He looked at his fist and saw Marcus' hand wrapped neatly around it. Marcus began to squeeze his hand and Percy started wincing in pain. He pushed down on Percy's hand and lowered it to the ground, bending his wrist. He let go and Percy grabbed his hand and rubbed it. He looked up at Marcus and then closed his eyes. Marcus leapt at him with his leg stuck straight out. He kicked Percy in the face and Percy fell over backwards into the grey mud. Marcus jumped on top of him and jammed his forearm into Percy's neck. He began crushing his throat with his weight and gritting his teeth out of anger. He jumped up and kicked Percy in the stomach, and grabbed Percy by the shoulders to sit him up. He put one hand under Percy's jaw. "You remember what my last words were?" Marcus whispered in his ear.

Percy opened his eyes wide in panic. "You're going to rip my fucking head off and shove it down my throat," Percy gasped.

"Unlike you, I keep my promises," Marcus said.

Marcus dug his fingers in under Percy's chin and began yanking on his head. Percy's head ripped right off of his neck and Marcus held it up for the crowd to see. He had a crazed look in his eyes and held it up high, whilst suddenly realising he was screaming with bloodthirst. Declan, Azazel and Timothy were standing on the edge of the crowd, watching in awe. Marcus had a hold of Percy's head in his hand, high up in the air, and with his other hand he had a hold of Percy's upper body. He turned his body around so as not to strain his neck, as he looked around at the faces of everyone around him, and then he plunged the head straight down into the neck of Percy's body. His gold wings shot up out of his back and he lifted straight up into the air. He threw Percy's body back to the ground, and the crowd of decayed angels and demons swarmed towards it as it turned to ash. He looked down at his hand and the Sword of the Angels instantly appeared. He looked down at Declan with a huge, crazy smile on his face. He flew off towards the cave where Beelzebub was. "Go get him," Declan said almost to himself.

Marcus landed on the edge of the entrance to the cave and stormed in. He walked past demons and devils that parted to let him past. They all stood very far back as they all knew who he was, and they all saw his wings. They knew that if he had his wings back, he had his power back. Marcus walked right up to the staircase that led up to where Beelzebub was sitting. He had his sword in his hand by his side, and with his other hand he pointed up the staircase at Beelzebub. "You!" he shouted, "You have to let me go."

Beelzebub sat forward and stared at Marcus with his sword in his hand, and his golden wings swaying above his head.

"And what's in it for me?" Beelzebub asked.

"You get to live!" Marcus shouted back. Marcus turned around and looked at all the demons and devils in the cave staring at him. "You all get to live," he said. He turned back and looked up at Beelzebub. "You just gotta let me go."

Beelzebub sat back in his chair and looked at Marcus with a question in his eyes. "You're in over your head," Beelzebub said.

"No," Marcus said, "I'm in over your head. Let me go, or you will die." Marcus walked up a few of the stairs. He stared into the devils big, black hate filled eyes. He had only ever come across him once before, but they both had a mark on each other to prove that they had crossed paths before. "You know the secret to resurrection, don't you?" Marcus asked.

"Why would you think that?" Beelzebub asked.

"Because Dorian came back, so there's obviously some way of coming back. Tell me."

"You think I will disclose that information? Why don't you just find out what it's like for yourself?" Beelzebub grinned.

Marcus turned around to talk to Beelzebub's minions. "Why do you all put up with his shit?" he shouted, "You could so easily have a better governed system under Heaven. Ever since this behemoth took over here, this place has become the end for everyone. Don't you want to go back to Hell? Or Heaven? Or even Earth?"

Four devils within the cave began slowly advancing on Marcus. There were still a few others that were staying still and were receded up against the wall. They seemed to not want any confrontation with Marcus, unlike the four others. He held out his sword and pointed it steadily at them in an attempt to discourage them. They hesitantly came closer as their mouths began to water. They stared at Marcus like he was breakfast, yet they were advancing slowly as they knew all too well what he was capable of. Their scaly wings rose up from their back in unison as they all leapt at him. He fell to his knees and rolled down the staircase underneath them with his sword swinging a high arc above him. It sliced through two of the devils as they burst into flames and disintegrated to ash. He rolled to his feet at the foot of the stairs as he caught his balance with a ready stance. The devils began flying around the cave in a clockwise motion, flying down to swoop at him. *Big mistake*, he thought. He ran around towards the first one coming for him, and flew head on towards it, slicing it clean in half in midair as the burst of flame surrounded him. He quickly diverted towards the ground and landed with a springy motion. In the same quick movement, he pounced off the ground, shooting straight up.

Marcus held his sword above his head and was aiming directly for a devil above him. The sword pierced straight through its stomach as he continued flying upwards. They both hit the roof with a loud thud, as small stones broke loose and fell to the cave floor. The devil, pinned to the rocky ceiling, let out a mighty roar as it erupted in flames. Marcus tore his sword out of the rocks and let himself fall towards the floor. He landed with one knee to the ground in a crouch, and his fist resting against the callused cave floor, his sword still firmly in his other hand. He looked up the staircase, straight at Beelzebub. Beelzebub raised his chin slightly, as if almost impressed. "Get him," he said softly.

Two more devils rushed up behind Marcus, who darted up the staircase and turned around swinging his sword, just in time to slice them both in half. The sword swung straight through their stomachs, as though they were butter. They burst into flames and disintegrated as flecks of ash fell to the floor. A sudden shock fell over Marcus' face. He felt a sharp pain in his back. He awkwardly turned around to see Beelzebub standing right behind him, with a dagger in his hand. The dagger was covered in Marcus' blood. He reached over his right shoulder with his left hand and touched his right shoulder blade. He felt the warm, sticky liquid pulsating out of his back with every heartbeat. Marcus knew this was it, as he pulled his hand back in front of his face and stared at his red fingers. His eyes moved back up to meet the eyes of Beelzebub. He was angry and fading fast, but he mustered the only word he could think of, "Coward".

He faced the foot of the stairs again and fell forward, landing face first on the steps below him. His sword bounced down the remaining steps. "Grab the sword!" Beelzebub shouted. The Sword of the Angels disappeared instantly. Marcus' body was lying inert on the steps with his head near the bottom, and his feet up near where Beelzebub was standing. Flames started to engulf Marcus as Beelzebub quickly put his hand out and the flames began to subside. Beelzebub had the ability to control fire, and it was the only element he was able to bend to his will. Angels used to be able to control certain elements, but since it weakened them drastically, God decreed that only the strongest of angels would be able to. None have been able to summon enough power to do it since. But, Beelzebub was strong enough to have control over fire, and he was the only one. He knelt down and put his hand on Marcus' back. The disintegration stopped instantly, and Marcus lay there, inert. Beelzebub looked down at the body. "Get rid of it," Beelzebub growled.

A devil stepped forward and inspected the body. "Where do you want me to put the body?" the devil asked.

"Dump it at the gates of Heaven. I want them to see for themselves," he said. Beelzebub walked back up the steps to his throne and sat down. He put his horny head in his hands and rubbed his face. The devil carried the body away and all the other demons and devils in the room looked up at Beelzebub. He took his hands away from his face and looked down at them all, staring at him. "What?" he shouted.

They all turned away from him and scattered.

CHAPTER VIII

Lucifer spotted a devil flying out of the gates of Purgatory before Ben did. The red figure in the distance grew larger as it got closer to them. It was carrying something in its arms, and it almost looked like a body. The devil started flying off course instead of coming straight for the gates, and swooped around, dropping Marcus' body just in front of Ben and Lucifer. It quickly diverted its course back towards Purgatory and flew as fast as it could. Ben and Lucifer quickly jumped up and ran over to Marcus' body. They checked it over and noticed the large wound in his back. Ben put one arm under Marcus' legs, and the other under his shoulders, and hoisted him up. Lucifer and Ben turned to run into the gates of Heaven. "Let us in! Quickly!" Lucifer shouted at Peter, the gate keeper.

Peter ran to the gates and opened them. Lucifer and Ben ran down the blue carpet-like floor to the steps where God was sitting. God stood up off of his throne as he saw them approaching. He noticed the lifeless body in Ben's arms and recognised it instantly. Ben fell to his knees with Marcus still in his arms. He took his arm out from underneath Marcus' legs and put it on his shoulder. "Marcus!" Ben shouted. There was no response. "Marcus!" Ben shouted again.

God walked down the steps to where Ben was with Marcus' body in his arms. Ben looked up at God. "He'll be okay, right?" Ben asked.

God sadly shook his head, "No".

The surrounding angels gasped in horror. There were a few small cries, almost like a high pitched yelp. None could believe what they had just heard. Ben looked up at God and stared into his eyes. He flared his nostrils as he breathed in deeply, and his eyebrows changed shape. They began pointing directly towards his nose. Anger began flooding his thoughts. "No…" he said.

God returned his stare, but with compassion and sorrow. "Yes, Ben. I'm sorry," God replied.

Ben stared even longer. He began breathing heavier. "No!" he shouted.

God let silence build up as he looked down at Ben, and Marcus' lifeless body. He felt the sadness throughout all of the Heavens, but most of all, he felt Ben's anger and pain. He kept his emotionless, stern face. "Ben, I feel your pain. I feel your disbelief. You need to accept this. Marcus has…"

"Bullshit!" Ben shouted, "You can fix this!"

"Ben!" Lucifer said, "watch your mouth!"

Ben lowered Marcus' body to the floor and stood up. "I don't care! He can fix this!"

"Ben, I can't fix this," God said.

"The almighty God can't even bring the most powerful angel back? You wrote it yourself. The most powerful sword must belong to the most powerful angel. If he's the most powerful angel, then why is he dead? What can you do then?" Ben questioned.

"Ben," Michael said, "You can't question God's power."

"I'll do whatever I want. I've been told my whole life that you are the be all and end all of power. I was brought up to believe that there was nothing that you couldn't do, and Marcus did nothing but reinstate that belief in me. As far as I'm concerned, there is no Heaven without him. Now, can you bring him back, or not?" Tears began flowing from Ben's eyes.

God stepped forward and wiped the tears from Ben's eyes. He put his hand on Ben's shoulder and blinked. His beautiful blue eyes almost sedated Ben. "I am the power that helps you to do things on your own," God said, "I can't bring Marcus back, and it saddens me just as much as you to know that he's gone. All I can do is help you overcome your grief. You will never get over this, but I can guarantee that you will become accustomed to it. He will always be there, within you."

Ben stared at God's blue eyes with a look of serenity on his face, but his eyes quickly turned back to anger and he shook himself away from God. "If you aren't going to do anything, then I'll have to," he said, as the tears began to flow again.

He reached down to Marcus and took the Amulet of the Shadows from around his neck, and fastened it around his own neck as he readied himself to storm out of Heaven towards the gates of Purgatory. Lucifer lunged himself at Ben and tackled him. They both fell to the ground. "What are you doing?" Ben shouted.

"I can't let you do it, Ben. Marcus couldn't even take him down. What chance do you think you've got?" Lucifer asked.

"Get off me!" Ben shouted, "I wish I never came here. I preferred my life before all of this."

Ben got up and ran toward the gates of Heaven. Lucifer tried to chase after him, but Michael grabbed his shoulder. "Let him go," God said, "This next lesson in his to learn alone."

Ben fled down the blue carpeted street of Heaven towards the entrance, and as he passed through the gates, he took one last lingering look down towards Marcus' body, and all the angels staring back at him. He wiped his eyes with his sleeve and turned to run, as he saw a figure standing in front of him. Elderly, with long silvery hair, a beard, and dressed in outdated clothing. Ben instantly recognised that it was Arus, and his anger changed to sadness again, knowing there could only be one reason Arus was there. He threw his arms around

Arus' chest and sobbed uncontrollably, as Arus rested a comforting hand on his shoulder. Ben stepped back and looked into the old warrior's blank eyes. "You're taking this harder than I am," Arus said, "He must have meant a great deal to you."

Ben looked down in sorrow, not knowing what to say. He fought a quiver of his lip and looked up at the angel that Marcus always wanted to become, as he realised Marcus would never achieve that goal. His anger returned. "How does hiding in a cave help? All his life, he wanted to be you. But he was better than you. He never knew it, but he was better than you'll ever be. He wasn't a coward."

Arus stepped up next to Ben and placed a hand on his shoulder. "You're grieving, so I'm going to let that slide. For now. Go, before I change my mind."

Ben angrily nodded and walked down the staircase to Devils Tower. He fell to his knees and screamed at the clouds. Tears streamed down his face as the clouds darkened. Rain began falling over the countryside around him as it coloured the stone formation he was kneeling on a darker grey. Ben fell forwards onto his hands, as if trying to fight a gag reflex. His whole body shook as the rain soaked him to the skin. His hair was plastered to his head as the rain covered his tears, whilst he closed his eyes and shook uncontrollably. He slowed his breathing as he knelt down further and rested his forehead on his arms. His backside stuck straight up as if he were praying. His anger subdued. Sadness had taken hold once again. He didn't know what to feel. Emotions were flooding him like he was feeling them all at once, and unsure which one to pick. Anger, sadness, confusion, fear, disgust; even happiness. He even felt himself smile at one point, and wondered why he had smiled. He realised it was the shock he was in that was causing his emotional breakdown. He slowly stood up and breathed heavily, looking out over the countryside, but, at the same time, not looking at anything at all. His tears had stopped and all he felt was numb, with his mouth slightly open, and the muscles in his face completely relaxed, like he was under a spell. He breathed again deeply and opened his gold wings, as he flew up into the air.

Arus began walking towards the gates as Peter stepped in front of him. "Raphael, you know you're not allowed..." Arus put his hand on Peters face and pushed him over as he continued walking. He stepped onto the blue carpet and kept his stride, as he walked towards Marcus' body. All the angels watched him without a word, and the silence was deafening. No one could know what Arus would do, as his face showed no emotion. He stopped as he neared Marcus' corpse, and stared down at his dead son for a long moment. Nobody spoke. Arus looked up at God. The stare lingered as they both showed no emotion. Old friends, with a wealth of history together, and a great respect for each other. Arus broke the silence. "Are you happy now?" God stayed silent. "Is this what you wanted?" God still remained silent.

"How did you know?" Lucifer asked.

Arus shifted his gaze over to Lucifer. "I see they let you back in."

"With this face? How could they not?"

Lucifer smirked, and Arus frowned at him. "You created sin."

"You created... people! The naughty way!" Lucifer retorted.

"You defied God!" Arus barked.

"You defied science!"

Lucifer turned his head and gave Michael a stupid, open mouthed grin, but Michael wasn't amused. Lucifer quickly changed his face back to serious and looked forward again. "Okay... shutting up." He tried not to smile and rolled his eyes. "You'd all be bored without me."

Arus reached up under his jacket and pulled out the Sword of the Angels. "Only one reason this would appear before me. The Commander of Battle chooses whom their sword will go to when they die. I hoped I would never receive it." Arus looked back up to God. "How many more lives must be lost before you end this? Hm? What's God's big plan? That blubbering mess of a broken down half-breed that just stormed out of here crying?"

"Let's not forget you're responsible for that half-breed," Michael said.

Arus smirked as he glanced at Michael. "Yes," he said as he looked back to God, "That was all my doing. I created the Nephilim, and protected the bloodline. Why? Because I had to, I guess. Didn't I?" He looked up at God who still showed no emotion. "Then I tasked Marcus with protecting the bloodline. Whilst trying to protect the child, Marcus kills a human, and all is found out. We stand trial, Marcus for murdering a human, and me, for creating the whole mess. But wait, the punishment for murdering a human is death. Sure, it was in defence of another, but I'm guessing that's just a grey area, right? So you write the Revelation to create a loophole, regain the sword, this sword. Bring the Nephilim back into our lives to assist us, only to lose our most dedicated soldier, and probably the best commander this army has ever seen. No offence Michael."

Michael put a nonchalant hand up. "None taken. I agree," he said.

"So, stricken with grief, the kid runs away now... Or to paraphrase, the angel will fall. Am I right? The angel will fall? That's the Nephilim, yes? I'm guessing he didn't leave on the best of terms, given what he just said to me. And let me guess, he will rise again with the great power he was destined to behold." The crowd gasped in realisation. "Yes," Arus said, "All me." Arus began to clap. "Bravo. You dangled this whole prophecy in front of Marcus to get what you wanted. He believed in it, and did everything that was asked of him. Look where that got him. What kind of sick and twisted incentive was that? You see this? This is all on you."

God stepped down to Arus and put a hand on his shoulder. Arus swatted the hand away, while the crowd couldn't take their eyes off the pair. His nostrils flared as he stared with anger in his eyes. God tried to put his hand back on Arus' shoulder, as Arus grabbed him by the wrist. "Don't," he said.

God blinked. He moved his hand towards Arus' shoulder effortlessly, as Arus strained to hold it away from him. God's hand stopped firmly on Arus' shoulder. "It is time we talked, old friend."

They both disappeared. Everyone began looking around, wondering where they had gone. God rarely ever transported out of Heaven; he never needed to. Lucifer bent down and picked up Marcus' body as he walked off to the side of the steps. The whole crowd followed him down the blue street that continued to the left. At the end was a large brazier, with waves of burning flames, glistening and illuminating the pearlescent buildings around them a fiery orange. Lucifer walked up to it and placed Marcus' body in the fire. "Farewell, dear brother." His body began to disintegrate and turn to ash, as the brazier and the wall behind it rotated out of sight.

Ben walked into his house and slammed the front door. He walked over to the kitchen bench and rested his elbows on it, and put his head in his hands. He wiped the tears from his eyes and walked through the kitchen and the hallway into his bedroom. He opened up the cupboard and took a suitcase down from inside it, and threw it on the bed. He opened the suitcase and started throwing some clothes into it. He zipped it up and pulled it off the bed, and turned and looked at the full length mirror in his wardrobe door. He was not the same person he was a few weeks ago. He was not even a person anymore. He had lost his humanity and he knew he could never get it back. He grabbed the handle of his suitcase and continued staring at his reflection as he screamed and swung the suitcase at the mirror, shattering it. He was instantly standing in a field in broad daylight, near a large church. The roof was curved and there was a large cross above the front door. It almost looked like a large aircraft hangar. He lugged his suitcase through the field until he came to a road. He turned left and began walking down the road. He saw houses on his right, and then the houses began on his left. He turned left at the next street and there was another right instantly. He looked up at the street sign and saw the name; Fenley Place.

Ben remembered it from his childhood, and remembered it being a lot taller. Of course, in his childhood, he was a lot smaller. He walked down the street past all the familiar houses and came to a bend in the road. He followed the road around and walked up towards a dead end. There were two gravel car parks at the dead end, and two driveways either side of them. The one on the right was paved, and the one on the left was brick. Both driveways curved towards two car garages at the end. He walked up the brick driveway on his left and turned left onto a brick path just before he reached the garage. The path led around a two storey house towards the front door underneath a small balcony. He reached the front door, and knocked on it quietly. It was a cream coloured door with two stained glass windows in it, both upright and side by side, like the Roman numeral for two. He saw a figure coming towards the door through the stained glass, and the front door opened. A smile fell across Ben's face. "Hi Dad," he said.

"Ben!" his father said, "What a nice surprise. It's good to see you, son!" They hugged. Ben's father stepped away and took a look at his fully grown son. He had a large smile on his face and his eyes showed nothing but happiness behind his glasses. He stood a little taller than Ben and a little broader, and he had short, black curly hair on top of his head. He was wearing a t-shirt and shorts, and had bare feet. Ben stepped inside and dumped his suitcase to the left of the door. The floor was tiled and to the right was a doorway to a spare bedroom, and to the left, the entranceway opened up into a lounge room. There was a set of double doors at the end of the entranceway that led to a living area with an open plan kitchen. There was another door on the right which led to the bathroom, and then a staircase off to the right that rotated in the middle to take you upstairs, so that you would turn a full 180 degrees to finish climbing the stairs. "Guess who's home!" Ben's father shouted.

Ben's mother peered out of the kitchen through the double doors and saw Ben standing in the entrance way with his father. "Ben!" she shouted, "I hope you didn't spend too much money coming over here."

"I didn't Mum, it's okay," Ben said.

"Do you have enough money? How long are you staying for? You don't look too happy, is everything okay?"

"Enough questions, I'm here. Can we leave it at that?" Ben said.
"Well it's good to see you," she said, as she gave him a hug.

Ben closed the front door and walked through the double doors and into the living area. He slumped himself onto the leather couch and sat backwards, resting his head on the back of the couch. His parents came and sat on the couch that ran at a right angle to the one Ben was sitting on. They both looked at him. He picked his head up off the back of the couch and looked at them. The TV on his right was playing some sort of home renovation show. Ben looked down at the tiled floor. "Marcus is dead," Ben said.

"Oh no, that's awful!" his mother said, "How?"

"He was stabbed in the back," Ben said.
"I always liked him. I told you New York was rough, didn't I?"

"Yes, you did. I just needed to get away, thought I'd come home."

"You didn't catch a taxi, did you?" his father asked.

"No, I made my way into the city and caught a train," Ben explained, "When I got here, I walked into town and caught a bus here."

"Okay, well you can stay in the spare room for now. How long are you planning on staying?" his mother asked.

"Not sure. Think I might stay for a while."
"What about all your stuff?" his father asked.

"My stuff is fine where it is for now. You got any scotch?"

"Don't just turn to alcohol to hide your grief." his father said.

"I'm not. I could just really use a drink right now. It's been a rough few days."

"You know where it is," his father said.

Ben got up off the couch and walked towards the kitchen. There was a large open bench in the middle of the kitchen with two sinks on it, and cupboards all around it. Ben opened the cupboard on the side that was facing away from the kitchen, and pulled out a black rectangular tin. He opened the tin and pulled out a bottle of Johnnie Walker Black label. He walked around the bench and opened another cupboard and pulled out a glass. He poured himself a drink and left the bottle on the bench. He stood there and took a sip as he stared out the back window in silence. "You're not going to put it away?" his father asked.

Ben glared at his father. His father saw the sadness in his eyes and nodded. "You're not going to put it away without pouring me one, are you?"

Ben took another sip of his drink. "You don't drink scotch. You've had that bottle in the cupboard for the past eight years and it's still about as full as when you gave me a try for my eighteenth birthday."
"Not very often, but I'll have one with you. I've been off the wine for a few days, so it'll probably blow my head off."

Ben sat his drink down on the bench in front of him and grabbed another glass to pour his father a drink. "Can you please get me a glass of wine?" his mother asked.

"Sure," Ben said.

He opened the cupboard above the oven and pulled out a wine glass, and then walked to the large stainless steel fridge next to the oven and pulled out a bottle of white wine. He unscrewed the cap and poured a glass of wine for his mother, and put the bottle back in the fridge, and then poured a glass of scotch for his father. He picked up all three glasses in both hands, like a professional drinker, and walked back to the living room and handed their drinks to them, put his drink on the coffee table, and sat down again. His father picked up a remote off of the coffee table and turned the TV off. He took a sip of his scotch. "Have you spoken to Marcus' family?" Ben's mother asked.

"I was with his brother when it happened, and his father came afterwards. He didn't seem too impressed. Lucifer took it well," Ben explained.

"Lucifer?" His parents both asked at the same time.

"That's what we call Marcus' brother. His name is Luke."

"That's a bit satanic," his father said.
"It's just a nickname, Dad," Ben lied.

"You've never mentioned Luke," his mother said.

"I only met him recently," Ben said, "He's actually really nice. He's always had such a bad reputation, but he and I have hit it off really well. We've actually become really good friends."

"Oh well that's nice," his mother said, "I'm sure God is taking good care of Marcus."

Ben coughed quickly. "God isn't doing anything for Marcus. There's nothing he can do."

"Why would you say a thing like that?" his mother asked.

"He can't bring him back, so how is he taking care of him?" Ben said.

"Of course he can't bring him back. But he will take care of him," his mother replied.

"Whatever," Ben muttered.

"You're dealing with grief, Benjamin. It's understandable that you're questioning God."

Ben shrugged. He didn't want to get into a religious debate. They had no idea what he was now, or what their entire family had been this whole time. He thought about it for a moment, and then wanted to forget. "Are there any movies on tonight?" Ben asked.

His father turned the TV back on. He flipped through the movie channels for Ben to see. "What do you feel like watching?"

"Anything," Ben said.

His father selected a movie and Ben rotated his body so that he was lying down on the couch with a clear view of the TV.

* * *

"Well I'm going to bed," Ben's mother said. The movie was nearly finished, and his mother had already fallen asleep halfway through it. She got up off the couch and bent over to kiss him on the forehead. "Goodnight. It's lovely to see you again." She walked up the stairs to go to bed.

Ben sat up and took the last sip of his glass of scotch. He got up and walked to the kitchen to pour himself another, and looked at his father as he was unscrewing the cap of the Johnnie Walker Black. "Can you keep a secret?" Ben asked.

His father turned the TV off. "Depends on the secret."

Ben poured himself a drink. "What if I told you that Marcus was an angel?"

"I'd tell you that you're drunk, and you should probably get some sleep."

They both laughed. Ben quickly composed himself. "I'm serious, Dad."

A serious look fell over his father's face. Ben knew what he was getting himself into. His father was very knowledgeable when it came to religion and the bible, and theology, and Ben wanted his father to believe in the things that he has seen. But as soon as he mentioned angels, he knew his father had an opinion. "Ben, I believe in angels. But I don't believe they walk among us and make themselves known to us. If Marcus told you he was an angel, I would have asked him for proof."

Ben took a sip of his drink at the bench and nodded. He walked back over to the couch and stood behind it. "What if he gave me proof?"

"Okay, so he gave you proof that he's an angel. So what? As I said Ben, I don't believe they walk among us and make themselves known to us. That's my own opinion, son. Like Clint Eastwood said, opinions are like arseholes, everybody has one."

Ben closed his eyes and let his gold wings seep out of his back. He opened his eyes just in time to watch his father's jaw drop. His father stood up and stared at the wings. They practically filled the entire room. His father stared into his eyes and looked down at the glass that Ben had in his hand. "I must be pissed," his father said.
"You're not drunk, Dad. This is real."

"You're an angel."

"I am now."

"How long have you been an angel?"

"For about two weeks now. Please don't tell Mum."

"Why not? She still goes to church. Why shouldn't I tell her?"
"Because I'm her baby boy. And she has a mouth like a lawn mower."

"That's not very nice. But I see your point. I can keep a secret." Ben's father stared up at the wings with happiness in his eyes. "They're so beautiful. I've always envisioned angels' wings like birds wings."

"Yeah, because feathers are so angelic," Ben laughed.

His father tilted his head to the side. "That wasn't funny."

Ben stopped laughing and thought on it for a second. He had finally understood why Marcus said it so often, and why Marcus found it funny, yet it still wasn't that funny. "No, it never was funny."

His father sat down again. "So, you were saying that Marcus is an angel."

"No, Marcus *was* an angel. Marcus is dead now, remember?"

"So he's in Heaven?" his father asked.

"No. There's Heaven, Hell, and this place we call Purgatory. When an angel is killed by a demon, they go to Purgatory. And when a demon is killed by an angel, they also go to Purgatory."

"So, Marcus is in Purgatory?" his father asked.

"No, let me finish."

"Okay, sorry."

"Marcus was killed by a demon, so he went to Purgatory. And then he was killed by the devil in Purgatory. When you're killed in Purgatory, you're gone for good."

"Marcus was killed by Lucifer?" his father asked.

"Um, okay," Ben said, "This is going to blow your head off, not the scotch." He paused for a second. "Marcus' brother is Lucifer."

His father sat back in shock. "Marcus was killed by his own brother?"

"Okay, Lucifer is the fallen angel, not the devil. The devil rules Purgatory, and Lucifer rules Hell. Two completely different entities. God actually forgave Lucifer last week and he's allowed back into Heaven now," Ben explained.

"Ben," his father said, "if you didn't have those gold things floating above your head right now, I'd have you committed. You know that, right?"

"I know that Dad," Ben said, "Which is another reason that we can't tell Mum. She's a celebrant, and she would preach, you know she would preach! There would be a lot at stake. There is a really big war coming between good and evil, and the last thing we need right now is publicity."

"You can understand that I'm finding this a little hard to come to terms with. I mean, my son is an angel. A *real live angel*. How do you understand something like that? I thought humans couldn't become angels."

"It's just something you'll have to get used to, and... there was a loophole," Ben said.

"I guess I'll have to," his father said, "So have you been to Heaven?"

"Yes, and it is beautiful. The buildings look like they're made out of pearl, and the streets look like blue carpet."

"And have you met God?"

"Yes, I met God. I actually yelled at him before I came here. He can't bring Marcus back. I didn't take that very well."

"Of course you didn't. That's grief. But hey, you needed someone to blame, right? I'll bet he gets that a lot. Some people need a scapegoat sometimes, and I'm sure that's part of his power, that he takes on all the pain. Hell of a burden. What's he like?"

"He is all that is beauty and peace. I was standing there with Marcus' body at my feet and tears streaming down my face, and he wiped my tears away and looked at me with such love in his eyes that all the pain almost disappeared. He told me that he can't bring Marcus back, and that all he can do is help me overcome my grief."
Ben let his wings seep back into his shoulders, and walked around the couch and sat on it. His back was facing the kitchen, and his father was on the couch at a right angle to the one he was sitting on, with his back facing the back wall of the house. "Well that's exactly right," his father said, "God isn't a miracle worker. Bringing Marcus back would be like raising the Titanic and saying it will sail again. I believe that God gives you the strength to do whatever you need to do. That is his ultimate power. This is all a learning curve for you. I would take anything he says as a blessing. If you ask him for the strength to overcome your grief, he will give it to you. That's just how powerful he is. So, how long have you known that Marcus was an angel?"

"Only about two weeks," Ben said, "Just before I became one."

"So you've known him all this time, and you only just found out?"
"Yes. We were visited by an angel that told me about Marcus not being allowed back into Heaven until he found his sword."

"His sword?" his father asked.

"Yes, Marcus is the commander of battle…" Ben stopped, took a deep breath and continued, "I mean, he *was* the commander of battle for the armies of Heaven. He had to find his sword on Earth before he was allowed back into Heaven."

"Let me guess," Ben's father said, "The sword at the entrance to Paradise."

"Correct," Ben said, "Marcus learnt that after I figured it out. Then all of a sudden, I'm in Hell meeting Lucifer and I have wings."

"Hell?" his father shouted.

"Shhh!" Ben said.

His father looked up the stairs, remembering Ben didn't want to tell his mother. "Sorry, but you've been to Hell?"

Ben nodded. "Unfortunately."

His father shook his head. "I don't even want to ask what that place is like."

Ben nodded again. "You don't want to know."
"So, your wings," his father said, "They're gold. They look amazing. So surreal."

"Yes, they're gold. I am a Seraph."

"Seraphim?" Ben's father asked, "Isn't that the highest?"

"Yes, it is. There's more to that story. You can tell an angel by the colour of his wings. All the different types have different colours. For instance, an angel has white wings. An archangel has light brown wings. A cherub has blue or red wings depending on which path they choose, whether that is a warrior, or a scholar. And Seraphim are gold." Ben explained.

"So if you've only been an angel for about two weeks, how can you be Seraphim?"

"Because there is a prophecy that speaks of an angel being born as a human, and becoming a Seraph straight away. I started off with white wings, and then they turned yellow. And after some training, they became fully gold. So now I am a Seraph."

"So the prophecy speaks of you?" his father asked.

"It's called the Revelation. It talks about Marcus finding his sword, the angel falling and rising again, and the human angel. The only problem is that the angel has fallen. How is he supposed to rise again if there is no coming back? Not even God can bring him back."

"Yes, but in writing this Revelation, God had a plan, right?" his father asked.

"Well, yes," Ben replied.

"So have a think about it. I think you'll be pleasantly surprised with the answer."

Ben tilted his head and looked at his father. "What do you mean?" he asked.
"I mean that not all religions are right, but not all religions are wrong, either," his father said, "Anyway, I'd better get to bed. You know where everything is. Make sure you turn all the lights off."

"I will. Thanks Dad."

"Goodnight."

His father went up the stairs and Ben was sitting on the couch all alone with his thoughts. He got up off the couch and walked towards the front door, and opened it to step out as he pulled a cigarette from his pocket. He put it in his mouth and pulled a lighter out of his jeans pocket, lit the cigarette and put the lighter away. He walked to the front of the lawn and looked out over the sea of bright lights in front of him. His thoughts began to race about what his father had said. *Pleasantly surprised...* By what? He almost remembered the Revelation word for word after only reading it once, as his mind tracked over every paragraph. He still didn't quite understand it. Unless... It was him that had fallen. He had left in anger, questioned God, renounced his angelic life. He wanted to go back to the way things were before. He had fallen. A sudden tear began to fall. He wasn't finished yet. He had to go back one day. He exhaled the toxic smoke and took a deep breath. For a moment, he felt he was home.

CHAPTER IV

Ben woke up the next afternoon and stared at the ceiling. He was in the spare room just inside the front door. He was lying on a large antique bed with a bed side table on each side of it. There was a circular table by the front wall to his left. The front wall was arched out from the rest of the room. The ceiling looked like a box with half a hexagon stuck on the top, and the three sides of the half hexagonal front had windows on each wall. The sun was shining through the windows. Ben got up out of bed and threw some clothes on and walked out of the room and through the entrance way into the kitchen. Past the bench in the middle of the kitchen was a long dining table. His father was sat at the far end eating lunch. "Afternoon," his father said.

Ben nodded and walked over to the cupboard. He stared in it for a long second and then closed the door and walked to the table. He sat down and rested his forearms on the table. "I have a surprise for you," Ben's father said.

Ben looked up at him. "What's that?" His father finished his lunch and took his plate around the bench and placed it in the dishwasher, then walked through the living room to a door that led to the garage. Ben stood up and followed him. They walked through the door into a small laundry with an open glass door on the left. They walked through the glass door and Ben's father pressed the button to the left, to open the garage door. There was a car in the garage with a large blue dust cover over it. His father began to pull off the dust cover and revealed the custom dark blue paint with two white stripes running from the front to the back. Ben stared at his old car with a big smile on his face. "The 1967 Shelby GT500 Fastback. Just as you left it," his father said.

Ben walked up to the front of the car and ran his hand along it, all the way to above the drivers' side door. He opened the door and sat in the car. His father walked up to the door and handed the keys to Ben. Ben took them and looked up at his father. "I thought you sold it."

His father smiled. "I figured you'd come back for it someday. Why don't you call it Marcus?"

Ben put the key in the ignition and started the engine. The motor purred in the small garage. "You going somewhere?" his father asked.

"Yeah, I'm gonna need money to pay for petrol. I suppose I should get a job. Might go see some old friends, too."

"Okay, have fun."

Ben pulled the glove box open and pulled out a few CD cases. He flicked through them and selected Brave New World by Iron Maiden. He took the CD out of the case and put it in the

CD player. He skipped through to track seven and the music pounded through the speakers. Ben pulled the car out of the garage and slowly drove it down the street. The singer began to sing about Azazel and demons, and Ben smiled. The chorus started and the lyrics spoke about it being the end of our world. Ben began to sing along about being the chosen one. "I knew I liked this song for a reason."

He came to the street that the church was on and turned the opposite way from the way he had walked from the day before. He came to a main road and checked for traffic. When the road was clear, he gunned the motor and turned right with a screech of the tires. He drove down the road and made a few turns and passed a supermarket. He turned right at a roundabout and made his way down the winding road. He turned right again and followed the road, around almost to the end. He turned into a driveway of a block of flats. He slowly cruised past the first few flats and came to a stop at the end of the driveway. There were two flats at the end of the driveway in front of him. He let the car idle, and gave it a very quick, loud, beefy rev, and sat there, waiting. The front door of the flat on the left opened and a man walked out. He was wearing a black Pearl Jam t-shirt and jeans. He was about Ben's age and had very curly hair on his head which was a mix of brown and blonde. He had a large grin on his face as he walked up to the drivers' side door of Ben's car. Ben wound down the window. "How long have you been back?" he asked.

Ben shut the engine off. "Just got back last night. How have you been, Ethan?"

"Pretty good. I thought your Dad sold this beast."

"So did I. Hop in."

"Okay, let me throw some shoes on," Ethan said as he turned to walk back into the flat. Ben sat and waited in the car. A moment later, Ethan walked out with a grey jacket on and walked around to the passenger side door. He jumped in the car and Ben started it up again. He reversed it out of the driveway and took off. Ethan looked around the inside of the car. It was the same as he remembered it. "I have always been so jealous of this car!" he shouted over the growl of the engine, "So what's been happening?"

"My best friend Marcus was killed, so I came home," Ben answered.

"Really? I'm sorry to hear," Ethan said, "Was that your friend that came with you last time you were here?"

"Yeah, that's him."

"Damn, he was pretty cool."

They drove on in silence for a few minutes. "Carly is pregnant," Ethan said.

"Are you serious?" Ben asked, "Congratulations! That's great. So you're gonna be a Daddy."

"Yep, it's still only the early stages, but I'm happy."

"That's great. I'm happy for you. It's strange, all these people I went to school with are getting married and having kids. I'm never gonna have kids," Ben said.

"Are you just saying that because that's what Alexandra used to say?" Ethan asked.

"No, I'm over that. It's been years." Ben pulled over and looked across the road at the house opposite them. "But I do still miss her. I wonder how she's doing," Ben said.

"I heard she got engaged. Sorry man."

"Like I said, I'm over it." The front door opened, and a young woman stepped out and looked at Ben's car. Ben stamped his foot on the accelerator and the car lurched out onto the road in a cloud of dust. "Did she see me?" Ben asked.

"It's not exactly the most common car, you know," Ethan said, "I'm pretty sure this is the only one in Huntington, and she knows cars."

"Yeah, I know."

"You want her back?" Ethan asked.

"No, I want her to be happy. As long as she's happy, I'll be happy," Ben said.

They drove into town and stopped outside the Scottish bar. They got out of the car and walked into the bar and sat down on a stool each at the bar. Nimrod was sitting at the end of the bar with a drink in front of him. He raised it to Ben. Ben nodded to him. "I'll be back in a second," Ben said, walking around to Nimrod and sitting down next to him. "We got him."

"I heard. Apparently you showed him no mercy."

"He got what was coming to him," Ben said.

"Yes, good job. Marcus would be proud."

Ben hung his head. "So you heard."

"Yes, we all did. I'm sorry Ben, I know you two were really good friends. He'd be proud of the angel that you've become."

"Thanks, that means a lot to me," Ben said, "Anyway, I'd better not keep my friend waiting."

"Good to see you again, kid," Nimrod said.

Ben walked back around to Ethan. "Who was that?" Ethan asked as Ben sat down.

"Just a friend of Marcus and mine. Thought I'd let him know the bad news."

"Fair enough, what are we drinking?" Ethan asked.

Ben looked up at the Johnnie Walker Blue on the shelf and then looked at the beer taps in front of him. There were four brass pipes sticking out of the bar with different names on the end of each tap. The bartender from the day before recognised Ben and walked over to them. "I'll just have a beer," Ben said.

"Make that two," Ethan said.

The bartender pulled two chilled glass mugs out of a gap in the bar and poured their beers. He sat them in front of Ben and Ethan and waited for the money to be handed over. Ben pulled out a fifty dollar note and handed it over. The bartender rung it up in the register and placed the change next to Ben's beer. "You got any jobs going?" Ben asked.

"Only in the kitchen. You interested in that?"

"I'll take any job at the moment," Ben said.

"I basically need someone to wash dishes and help prepare food."

"Sounds good to me," Ben said, "Do you want a resume or anything?"

"I wouldn't worry about it. If you need a job, you can have one. Plus, your new buddy over there said you're a very hard worker. Said you're on the ball and that he liked your work ethics. That's good enough for me."

"Okay, thanks. When do I start?" Ben asked.

"You can start tomorrow if you want. It's a Sunday, but we have a private function in here, so there will be lots of dishes to do."

"Done," Ben said, "I'll be here tomorrow."

"Be here at midday," the bartender said as he walked away.

"You feel like going out tonight?" Ethan asked.

"Maybe, not sure how much fun I'll be though."

"Oh come on, it'll be good for you."

"Ok, I'll go out."

"I'll just have to tell Carly," Ethan said.

"You think she'll let you go out?" Ben asked.

"Yeah, she's pretty easy going."

They both took a sip of their beer. Ben put his glass down on the bar and rotated it so that the handle was parallel with the edge of the bar. "So where are we going tonight then?" Ben asked.

"How about Finley's?" Ethan said.

"I haven't been there in a few years, guess that would be okay." Ben said.

They finished their beers and walked back out to the car. Ben jumped in and started it up, then leaned over and lifted the latch to unlock the door for Ethan. They took off and drove slowly through the town of Huntington. Ethan was pointing out things that have changed since Ben was last there. They made their way back to Ben's parents' house and as they pulled around the curve of the street towards the house, Ben slowed the car to a stop. "What are you doing?" Ethan asked.

Ben stared at the two car parks at the end of the street. There was a recent model silver Chevrolet in the slot closest to Ben's parents' house. He recognised it instantly. Ethan followed his gaze and recognised the car. "Alex is here," Ethan said.

"Really? I didn't notice," Ben said sarcastically. He pushed a small button on the dash and the garage door began to open. He pulled his car into the garage and hesitantly hopped out. Ethan crawled out of his door and noticed that Ben's body language showed that he was uncomfortable. They both walked through the laundry and into the living room. Alexandra and Ben's parents all looked up at him. Alex had long brown hair and was wearing tight blue jeans with a black t-shirt. She was sat on the couch Ben sat on the night before, and his parents were in the same place they were the night before. Alex stood up and stared at Ben with apologetic eyes. She walked around the coffee table to Ben and threw her arms around him. "I'm sorry to hear about Marcus," she said.

He left his arms limp by his side. At the last second, he put one arm around her lower back. She let go and looked at him. "It's so good to see you again," she said.

"You too," Ben said.

Ethan cleared his throat. "It's good to see you too," Alex said, "How's Carly?"

"Pregnant," Ethan said.

"Oh, congratulations," Alex said.

"I'd better take Ethan home; we're going out tonight and he should spend some time sucking up to see if he can come," Ben said.

"I'd better be heading off anyway," Alex said, "Are you free tonight?"

"I just said I'm going out," Ben said.

"No, I mean before that," Alex said.

"Yeah I guess so," Ben said, "I'll walk you out." They walked towards the front door.

"It was good to see you again guys," Alex shouted back to Ben's parents.

"Bye Alex!" Ben's parents shouted back.

Ben opened the front door and moved away so that Alex could walk out in front of him. He closed the door behind him as he stepped out. "It really is good to see you again," Alex said, "Are you sure you want to catch up tonight?"

"Yeah, I'd like that," Ben said.

"You seem a bit uncomfortable," Alex said.

"Alex, I just lost my best friend. How am I supposed to be?"

"Okay, I'm sorry. You want to pick me up at about six?"

"I can do that. I'll see you then."

Alex leaned over and gave him a kiss on the cheek. She grabbed the palm of his hand at the same time and slowly slid her fingers down to his until she let go. She walked away backwards with a lingering look at him and then turned to walk towards her car. She got in her car and reversed out of the park, and then turned backwards into the driveway and slowly took off. She gave Ben a small wave as she drove away. Ethan opened the front door and stepped outside. He looked over at Ben. "So you're going to catch up with her?" Ethan asked.

"I'm gonna have dinner with her," Ben said.

"See if sparks will fly?" Ethan said.

"No, I can't," Ben said.

"Why not?"

"It's complicated," Ben said.

CHAPTER X

After taking Ethan home, Ben parked his car in the garage and walked inside and to the spare room. He threw his suitcase on the bed and sifted through it for some clothes. He found a nice button up shirt and some black designer jeans, and threw them on the bed and walked into the bathroom and had a shower. He dried himself off and put the clothes that he put aside on, and then inspected himself in the full length mirror in the spare room and gave himself a nod of approval. He checked his watch and grabbed his keys off the table near the front of the room, and walked out to his car, started it up and edged out of the garage to drive to Alex's house. He pulled into the driveway just as she walked out of the house and sat in the passenger seat. She looked over at him with a smile. She looked amazing. She had a long silver dress on, and her hair was straightened. Her eyes showed so much happiness that it made Ben smile. "So, where are you taking me?" she asked with a smile on her face.

"I thought I'd take you somewhere familiar," Ben said. His memory recalled the first time he and Alex went out for dinner. They were sitting in the restaurant and eating their food, and talking most of the evening with a heightened sense of nervousness. Ben remembered sitting at the bar with her afterwards and trying to silence the voice in his head when Alex asked what he was doing. He told her that he had this voice in the back of his head that tells him to do things he probably shouldn't do, and when she asked him what the voice was saying, he kissed her. She told him that he should listen to that voice more often. He came back to reality and looked over at Alex with great emotion. She noticed the look in his eyes.

"You look like you did on our first date," she said. Ben looked away shyly. He and Alex were together for a long time before they broke up, and she was responsible for his intuition at knowing things in advance. He pulled out of the driveway and drove into town with so many thoughts running through his head. He remembered standing in the church with Marcus and Eran, and figuring out where Marcus' sword was. He owed a lot of his logical thinking to Alex. He looked over at her and smiled. He pulled into the car park at Mac's Steakhouse on the east side of town and switched the car off. He quickly jumped out of the car and ran around it to open Alex's door for her. "Still such a gentleman," she said, "This brings back memories."

"Yes, but unfortunately that voice in my head doesn't speak all that much anymore," he lied.

"That's a shame," Alex said.

They walked in through the front doors and were seated instantly. They picked up the menus on the table and had a look through them. "You look really good, Alex," Ben said.

"Thank you. So do you," Alex said, "You actually look younger."

Ben laughed. "Please, I'll always look fifteen."

Alex laughed. The waiter came over to take their orders and Ben ordered a steak with chips only, and Alex ordered a stuffed chicken breast with a side of vegetables. They gave their drink orders, and both blushed at the fact that they'd ordered the exact same meals as on their first date. The waiter brought their drinks over and they continued talking. "So, do you think you'll stay this time?" Alex asked.

"You say that like I left you," Ben said.

Alex looked down at the table. "I'm sorry," Ben said, "I'd be lying if I said I hadn't missed you."

"I've missed you too," Alex said.

"How does your fiancé feel about that?" Ben asked.

Alex shifted her weight on the seat. She gave Ben a reserved look. "We've broken up. He was too insecure. Always thinking that I was going out and picking up guys and then coming home at 5am after a night with someone else, when I was either working, or out with girlfriends. You were never worried about that, I always liked that about you."

"Obviously not enough," Ben said quietly.

"You're still bitter, aren't you?" Alex asked.

"I'm sorry," Ben said, "I'm not in the best frame of mind right now. So many things have happened over the past few weeks that have absolutely blown my mind; not to mention that I'll never see my best friend again. I stood there with his lifeless body in my arms and just felt like everything was falling apart. It's why I came home."

"I don't know what you're going through, so I can't understand it. But you can't treat people badly and blame it on your grief. I know that's a harsh thing to say, but I think you've known me long enough to know that I speak my mind," Alex said.

Ben took a sip of his drink. "You're right. I'm sorry. I just wish I knew how things are going to turn out."

"You will never know. That's what creates the element of surprise," Alex said.

Their meals arrived and they began to eat. They talked between mouthfuls about Marcus, and how long Ben was thinking about staying. Alex put her hand on Ben's. "You know I can't help but wonder where this is going," Alex said.

Ben looked into Alex's eyes and saw that she was truly happy to see him. "You're really happy I came back, aren't you?" he asked.

"Yes," she said, "I am. When I saw your car pull up today my heart started beating furiously. I just thought it was because I was nervous about seeing you, but when you took off, I thought that seeing you would make me feel better. And it really has."

Ben looked down at his plate and moved the chips around with his fork. "It's been good seeing you again too," he said.

They finished their meals and the waiter came to take the plates away. "Do you want to go sit at the bar?" Alex asked.

"I'd prefer it if we didn't," Ben said, "Just seeing you has brought back a whole lot of great memories, and also some that I hoped I'd forgotten."

"I'm sorry," Alex said, "for what it's worth."

"Do you want to come out with Ethan and me tonight?" Ben asked.

"Ethan and I," Alex corrected him.

Ben stopped in thought. "No, Ethan and me," he said.

Alex looked in confusion. "Take Ethan out of the sentence, it would just be, 'do you want to come out with me tonight?' You wouldn't say, 'do you want to come out with I tonight?', would you? Therefore, it's Ethan, and me."

Alex was gobsmacked. She had been corrected by Ben. A rare occurrence. "My, you've changed," Alex said, "and yes, I'd love to. Where are you going?"

"Maybe Finley's," Ben said.

"I'll be there. I can meet you there," Alex said with a smile.

"Okay, great," Ben said.

They walked up to the bar and Ben pulled out his credit card to pay for the meals. The waiter charged the card and wished them a lovely evening. They walked out the front door and Alex grabbed a hold of Ben's hand. He took a deep breath and looked down at their hands. Alex took her hand away. "Sorry," she said, "Old habits. I just feel so comfortable with you."

"It's okay," Ben said.

They hopped in the car and Ben drove Alex home. He drove home and had a lie down on his bed for a few hours, then drove to Ethan's house and picked him up, and they drove straight into town, to Finley's on Green Street. They got out of the car and walked to the front door. There was a small queue and Ben and Ethan went to line up, when Ben saw Nimrod standing at the door with a number around his neck. "Ben!" Nimrod called, "Come to this side of the ropes."

They stepped out of the line and walked around to the other side of the ropes, and Nimrod pulled the rope aside to let them in. They shook hands and Nimrod let them past into the entrance foyer. There was a rail in front of them, and past it was a flight of stairs beginning at their right, and going underground to their left. They walked around the railing and descended down the stairs. Nimrod waved at the bouncer at the bottom of the stairs and held up two fingers. The bouncer at the bottom was an older gentleman, sitting on a stool. He had a shaved bald head and a greyish-white goatee that hung down past his chin. He nodded to Nimrod, and put up two fingers to a girl standing behind a cash register at the bottom of the stairs. She nodded and waved Ben and Ethan through. They walked through a set of doors and saw a band on the stage in front of them, with a large crowd jumping up and down in front of the stage. Ben walked to his right and leaned his elbows on the bar, waiting to be served. He pulled out his wallet and pulled out a twenty dollar note, and looked at Ethan who had just walked up beside him. "What do you want?" Ben asked.

"Just a beer," Ethan said.

Ben ordered a scotch and a beer, and handed over the twenty dollar note. The girl behind the bar poured their drinks and sat them in front of Ben, and gave him his change. Ben handed Ethan his drink and picked up his own, as he turned around to look at the crowd. He saw Alex rushing towards them with a large smile on her face. She threw her arms around Ben and planted a big kiss on his lips. "Hey stranger!" she shouted over the music.

"Hey, how long have you been here?" Ben asked.

"About half an hour, "she said.

"Oh shit," Ethan said.

"What?" Ben asked.

"It's Carly's ex-boyfriend. Apparently he wants to kill me," Ethan said.

"That's not gonna happen," Ben said.

"Says you!" Ethan said, "The guy is a black belt or something."

"So what?" Ben said, "He doesn't look all that tough."

Ben looked Carly's ex-boyfriend up and down and caught his eyes. The man returned Ben's stare and glanced over at Ethan. He puffed up his chest and charged his way over. He stood right in front of Ethan. "What did you tell him about me?" he said to Ethan.

"Nothing, why?" Ethan asked.

"He's staring at me like he needs a good beating," the man said.

Ben snorted a small laugh out of his nose. "What's so funny?" the man asked.

"Nothing," Ben said, "I just find it funny that you're telling all of this to him and not me."

"Well he's the one that needs a beating!" the man shouted at Ben.

Ben slowly put his drink on the bar. The man pulled his shoulder back and lunged at Ethan with a mighty punch. Ben reached forward and slapped his palm around the man's fist. The man jumped at the shock of his powerful punch being caught by someone who didn't even look old enough to be in a pub. Ben twisted the man's arm around his back and pushed his hand up in between his shoulder blades. He grabbed the man by the back of his shirt and slammed his head into the bar. The man fell over unconscious. Three bouncers ran up to stop it, as Ben pointed to the man on the floor. Nimrod was amongst them. "He threw a punch at my friend. I just stopped him," Ben said.

The two other bouncers looked at Ben, and then at Nimrod. Nimrod nodded. "Thanks Ben, good work," Nimrod said.

The two other bouncers picked up the unconscious man and dragged him out the doors and up the stairs. Ben turned around and picked up his drink from the bar, and took a small sip. Alex and Ethan stared at him in disbelief. "What?" he asked.

"How did you do that?" Ethan asked.

"Do what?"

"You grabbed his fist in midair. It was like he had punched a wall. That was incredible," Alex said.

"It was nothing," Ben said.

"That was awesome!" Ethan shouted with a smile, "You completely smashed his head into the bar."

Alex half frowned at Ben. "I don't remember you being so violent," she said.

"Times change," Ben said.

He took another sip of his drink. He looked down at Alex's hands and noticed she didn't have a drink. He brought his other hand up to his mouth and made a drinking motion with it, as he lifted his eyebrows to ask if she wanted a drink. She nodded with a smile. He turned around to the bar again and pulled another twenty out of his wallet. He asked the bartender for a Malibu and soda water with plenty of ice. Alex smiled at the fact that Ben had remembered exactly what she drinks. The bartender brought the drink over and Ben handed it to Alex. He grabbed a straw from a glass tumbler full of fresh straws on the bar, and put it in the drink for her. Her smile grew wider. Ben moved around the bar a little until he was next to the wall. There was a small wooden box next to him, and standing on the box was Nimrod. He was a short man, and it was almost as if he needed to stand on the box to look over the crowd. Ben was resting his elbows on the bar with his drink in one hand. Alex was standing just to his right, facing away from the bar. A look of shock hit her face.

A finger tapped Ben on the shoulder. Ben turned around just in time to see a fist coming towards his face. He ducked quickly and grabbed the arm that the fist belonged to. He reached forward and grabbed hold of a man and threw him against the bar. "What" he shouted.

The man put both of his arms up and looked terrified. He flinched, thinking that Ben was about to hit him. "I'm sorry," he begged, "I was just defending my friend."

"Your friend that started the fight before?" Ben asked angrily.

"Well, yeah," the man said, "That's his ex-girlfriend's boyfriend, right?"

"That's right. His *ex-girlfriend*. Make sure he gets that message too, alright?" Ben said, as he tapped the man on the forehead with his middle finger. He stepped away from the man and let him walk away. Nimrod looked down at Ben from his box. "You start another fight, and I'll have to get you to leave. You know that, right?" Nimrod asked.

"I haven't started any fights. You saw that with your own eyes," Ben said.

"Yes, but you're the centre of attention now, so if anything starts now, it'll be your fault. I told you this place was going to hell."

"Hell?" Ethan questioned, "This place has become worse than hell."

Ben looked quizzically at Ethan. "How would you know? You've never been to Hell," he said gruffly.

"And you have?" Alex asked.

Ben leaned over to Alex's ear. "Don't ask questions that you don't want answered."

She shook her head in shock and looked at him strangely, as Ben took another sip of his drink. She twisted the straw in her drink around towards her mouth, and took a sip. She looked up at Ben and leaned over to his ear. "Can you give me a ride home?"

"We'll have to get Ethan a taxi," Ben said, "I've only got two seats, the back ones were taken out, remember?"

They both looked over at Ethan. Ben walked up to him and put his mouth right next to his ear. Ethan leaned over to listen. "Is it alright if you get a cab home?" Ben asked.

Ethan looked at him wryly, and then looked at Alex staring at the two of them. He smirked. "That's my boy," Ethan said, "More than happy to, my friend."

"Thank you," Ben said. He walked back to the bar and nodded to Alex, and she smiled. Ben drank the last of his drink in one gulp and looked at Alex. "You want to go now?"

"Yeah, I'm not really in the mood to be here," she said.

Ben reached over and tapped Ethan on the shoulder. Ethan turned around to look at them. "You want to go now?" Ben asked.

Ethan didn't hear the words but saw his lips move and figured out what he was saying. He nodded and Ben turned around to shake Nimrod's hand. "I'll see you later," Ben said.

Nimrod nodded. "You better come get me when the battle begins," Nimrod said.

"I will." Ben said, "It would be an honour to fight beside you."

They gave each other a small smile and Ben turned to walk away. Alex and Ethan followed him. They walked up the stairs and out of the foyer into the cold night air. There were two cabs parked just outside the front door. Ben and Alex walked Ethan over to the taxi, and Ben opened the door for him. "Have a good night man," Ben said.

"Thanks champ," Ethan said, as Ben closed the door.

The taxi pulled away from the curb and Alex and Ben began walking down the street towards the small alley where he parked his car. He didn't like parking it on a busy street, as it attracted enough attention as it was. They turned into the alley and heard a woman screaming. Ben looked up the alley and saw a man crouched over a woman in a shadow. Ben's sword immediately appeared in his hand and he rushed towards the man. He pulled him off of the woman and held him up against the wall. The man's face began to change shape and Ben looked at him with shock. He realised that it was a demon and thrust his blade through its stomach. The demon burst into ichor and settled on the ground. The woman stood up and looked at Ben. "Thank you," she stuttered, as she turned and ran away.

Alex walked up to Ben's side and looked down at the puddle. She looked up at Ben in awe and wrapped her arms around his elbow. He let the sword in his other hand disappear. "What is going on, Ben?"

"You wouldn't believe me if I told you," Ben said.

They drove back to Alex's house and Ben parked in the driveway. He hopped out and opened up her door for her as she stepped out of the car gracefully. She smiled at him and walked towards her front door. She pulled her keys out of her bag and put one of them in the lock on the door. She opened it without saying a word and walked inside, leaving the door open. She stood there holding the door and waiting for Ben to walk in after her. He stepped inside the familiar house as she closed the door and turned on the light. He saw the staircase that led up to the lounge and kitchen ahead of him. Alex walked up the stairs and he followed her. She flicked light switches as she got upstairs, walked to her right and sat down on the couch, breathing a deep breath. She looked up at him standing in the doorway between the lounge room and the entrance to the kitchen. "Sit down."
It was a big room with a high ceiling. He looked around and walked over to the couch to sit down next to her. She moved

towards him and rested her head in his lap. "Can you stay here tonight?" she asked.

Ben took a deep breath and looked down at her. She rotated her body so that she was looking straight up at him. "I probably shouldn't," he said, "but if you really want me to, I can."

"I want you to. I just feel so comfortable around you, and it would be nice to have you here."

"Okay, I'll stay."

Alex half frowned and looked at him. "What is it?" he asked.

"What happened tonight?"

"What do you mean?"

"You were so confident in your fighting, and then in the alleyway. What was that?"

Ben sighed. "I shouldn't really be showing you this." His gold wings began to seep out of his back. She looked up above him and sat up instantly. Her jaw dropped and her eyes showed that she was in complete awe of what she was looking at.

"What the hell is that?" she asked.

"Alex," Ben said, "I'm an angel."

She looked him in the eyes and almost began to laugh when she saw that he was serious. She knew the look in his eyes, and she could always tell when he was mucking around. This time he wasn't. She composed herself and stared straight into his eyes. "How long have you been an angel?"

"For about two weeks now," Ben said, "Marcus was an angel too."

"But you said he died," Alex said.

"He did die," Ben explained, "He was killed by the devil."

Alex looked at the floor, wondering whether to believe him or not. She looked back up at his wings and then decided that he was telling the truth. He lied to her once before at the beginning of their relationship and told her he would never do it again. To this day, he hadn't told her a single lie. She looked back into his eyes. "So that's what you meant by not asking questions that I don't want answered."

"Yes," Ben said, "that's right."

She looked him up and down. "So, that means that you actually have been to Hell?"

"I have," Ben said.

They stayed silent for a while. Alex was staring at the floor like it was telling her a story. Ben looked at her with disappointment. She looked into his eyes. "What's wrong?" she asked.

"It's stupid," Ben said.

"Tell me," Alex said.

"Well, I really want to be with you, but I can't."

"Why not?"

"I'm an angel, Alex. I'm not a human anymore," he explained.

"You know," Alex said, "I never used to believe in all that stuff."

"Well it's a bit hard now, considering your ex-boyfriend is an angel," Ben said.

"Good point. So that's why you were so fearless at Finley's."

"Humans don't really scare me all that much anymore," Ben said.

"What about in the alley?" Alex asked.

"That was a demon," Ben said.

"What?"

"A demon. It looked like it was trying to hurt that poor girl. She's lucky we showed up when we did."

"This is all just a little too much for me," Alex said.

"I didn't expect you to understand, and I wish there was some way that you and I could work. But I'm afraid that I'm not allowed to be involved with a human. That's why Marcus' dad was exiled from Heaven."

"What do you mean?" Alex asked.

"Marcus' dad fell in love with a human, and he was forced to retire his position." Ben explained.

"What position?" Alex asked.

"He was the commander of battle for the armies of Heaven. He fell in love with a human and was forced to retire, and then Marcus had to take up the position."

Alex rested her head in his lap again and looked up into his eyes. Her eyes wandered above his head to his golden wings floating above him, and she gave a small smile. "What are you smiling at?" Ben asked.

"I have my own guardian angel," she said, as she wrapped her arms around his waist.

He breathed a small sigh and rested his head against the back of the couch. "Don't you have to go back to Heaven?" she asked.

"I don't think I really can go back," Ben said.

"Why not?"

He hesitated for a second. "I kind of questioned God's power and went crazy at him."

"So what will you do then?" Alex asked him.

"I guess I'll just have to take every day as it comes. From what I've seen, angels don't age. So in thirty years' time, I'll still look like this. I think people are going to notice that. I'll probably end up going back to New York."

"But why?"

"I can't stay here, Alex. I can't make this very public, and eventually I'm going to have to give some reason why I still look twenty-five, while everyone else is getting older. Everyone knows me here."

"Have you told your parents?" Alex asked.

"Dad knows. I haven't told Mum yet, but she'll figure that something is up. I've realised tonight that I'm going to have to tell her. My whole family will have to know." Alex nodded. "In a way, I'm dead. I can't do anything a normal person could do. I can't even become a father, anymore. My life as a human is over."

Alex looked up at him for a second, as her nerves began to race. "Ben, I have to show you something," Alex said.

"What?" Ben asked.

Alex walked over to the cabinet the TV was sitting on and opened the cupboard. She pulled out a photo album and flicked through the pages. She sat down next to him and pulled out a photograph and handed it to Ben. He took it and looked at it closely. It was a photo of Alex and her parents. Her father was holding a small child. He looked to be about two years old. "Who's the kid?" Ben asked.

"Well, that's what I wanted to show you," Alex said hesitantly.

"Yeah? Who's is he?"

Alex looked into Ben's eyes. "He's yours."

Ben looked a little closer at the photo, as his eyes opened as far as they would go. The boy in the photo looked just like he did as a child. He almost didn't hear Alex when she told him he was his, and he was trying to remember what she had said, thinking that he may have misheard her. But, he could tell by looking at the photo that what he thought he had heard her say, was accurate. He let his wings seep into his back as he looked over at Alex. "Why didn't you tell me?"

"How could I, Ben?" she said, "We broke up and you just left."

"What's his name?" Ben asked.

"William," Alex said, "William Benjamin Waters."

A tear fell from Ben's eye. It slowly trickled down his face and landed on the photo right on top of his sons face. "But, that was my grandfathers' name."

"And the name that you always said you would name your son."

"Where is he?" Ben asked.

"He's asleep in the other room with mum," Alex said, "She stayed here to baby-sit for me. Do you want to see him?"

"Yes, I do," he said.

Alex stood up and walked behind the couch into the hallway. Ben followed her as she went into the door at the end of the hallway. Alex's mother was lying asleep on a queen size bed with William beside her. He was fast asleep. Ben walked over to the edge of the bed, as Alex put a finger up to her mouth. He put his hand on his sons forehead and ran his fingers through his hair. Alex's mother opened her eyes and looked at Ben with a smile. "Hi Ben," she whispered. Ben nodded a hello. He gently kissed William on the forehead and stood up. He walked backwards out of the room, staring at his son.

Alex closed the door behind her, and they walked back into the lounge room and sat on the couch. Ben stared at the wall. "When William asks where his Dad is, what am I supposed to tell him?" she asked.

Ben put his hand up to his chest and tapped on his heart with two curled fingers. "Tell him I'm in here, and always will be," he said.

Tears began to fall from Alex's eyes. She leaned over and kissed him. "Just promise that you'll visit us. Come on, let's get some sleep." She grabbed his hand and led him to the bedroom.

CHAPTER XI

Ben woke up and looked around the room. He remembered being there three years earlier, and not one single thing had changed except for the photographs in the frames on the chest of drawers at the far end of the room. He noticed that they were all of Alex and William. There was one frame that was empty. Ben guessed that it used to contain a photo of the ex-fiancé, as it once held a photo with Ben, himself in it. He looked to his right and noticed that Alex wasn't there. He slowly pulled himself out of bed and slipped his jeans on, and walked out to the lounge room to see Alex sitting on the floor tickling William, who was laughing hysterically. He looked at the two of them and smiled. Alex looked up and saw the smile on his face. William looked up at him and his face changed to serious. He looked up at Alex and stood up and moved closer to her. He turned around and put his mouth to her ear. "Mummy, is that the angel?" he whispered.

"Yes Will, that's the angel," Alex said, "That's your Daddy."

A tear ran down Ben's cheek. He squatted down as William slowly turned back around towards him. "If you're really nice to him, he might show you his wings," Alex said.

William slowly walked up to Ben and poked his cheek. He then put both of his palms on Ben's cheeks and turned his head around, while still holding onto Ben's face. "He doesn't look like an angel," he said. He pronounced 'L' as 'W' so it sounded like he said *wook wike*. Ben let his wings seep out of his back as he stood up. William turned around and saw the wings floating in the air above Ben's head. He turned and looked at Alex with a large boyish smile on his face. "I have to work at twelve," Ben said.

Alex stood up. "What time will you finish?"

"Not sure, late afternoon maybe," Ben replied.

"Okay," Alex said, "You can come back here if you like."

"I'd love to," Ben said.

Alex's mother walked into the room and stepped back when she saw Ben's wings. "What on earth is that?" she shrieked.

"It's okay," Alex said to Ben, "I'll explain it to her."

Ben let his wings seep into his back. "Always lovely to see you Marie." Ben walked back into the bedroom and put on his shoes. He saw William standing in the doorway looking at him. He smiled at William, who then ran up to Ben and wrapped his arms around him. "Can you keep a secret?" Ben asked him. William nodded and looked into his father's eyes.

"Good, you mustn't tell anybody that I'm an angel, okay? It's our little secret." William nodded with a big smile and hugged Ben again. "Bye Will," Ben said, "I'll be back later."

Ben stood up and walked out of the room, as William followed. He gave Alex a small kiss on the cheek and walked down the steps and out the front door. He jumped in his car and started the engine, staring at the steering wheel. He was a father and he never even knew it. Almost four whole years. He began to regret that he'd left for New York. He had missed so many things. Birthdays, first steps, Christmas's; he had to make up for lost time. He had a son. His whole world had once again, completely changed. Something he always wanted, had somehow always been there. He had a new priority. From the moment he saw his son lying on the bed asleep, he fell in love instantly. The feeling was something he had never known before. He took a long look at the house and pulled out of the driveway. He drove home and looked around for his parents. Surely they knew. Why didn't they tell him? He found them both out in the backyard, doing some yard maintenance. "Why didn't you tell me?" he asked.

They both looked at him, guiltily. They knew exactly what he was talking about. "It wasn't our news to tell, Ben."

Ben frowned. "Not even a phone call? Hey Ben, you're a father. Congratulations."

"We wanted to tell you," his father said, "But she wanted to show you for herself. She begged us not to. We weren't happy about it, but we respected her wishes. You know now, don't you?"

Ben was aflame with emotions. He wasn't sure whether to be happy or angry. Both of his parents stopped what they were doing and walked over to him. They moved around to get into his eyesight, as he was staring into nothingness. They looked at him, both with smiles on their faces. "Congratulations, Ben," his mother said, "you're a father."

He fell towards them in a hug, one arm around each of them, as he began to sob. They were happy tears, but still, he was filled with regret about what he had missed. He stepped back, and out of the hug. "I swear, from this day on, I will not miss one birthday, one Christmas, any event. I will be here for him, always."

His mother smiled. "He is such a beautiful boy. I know you will be an amazing father."

Ben finally smiled. "Thanks, Mum. I gotta get ready for work. We'll talk later."

They both nodded. His father gave him a tap on the shoulder as a gesture of pride. He was proud of his son. Ben went inside and got ready for work. He put on a black t-shirt and jeans, and threw his black jacket over the top. He jumped back in his car and drove to the Scottish bar. He walked up the steps and through the front door. The bartender looked up from the bar and smiled. "You're early," he said to Ben.

"I find it's better to show up early on the first day to see what you're in for," Ben replied.

"That's a very good attitude. Come through to the kitchen."

Ben walked through the gap in the bar and followed the bartender through a doorway to the kitchen. "I'm Danny," the bartender said. He pointed to a small chef who looked to be in his early fifties. "That's Joseph. Joe, this is… umm, what did you tell me your name was?"

"I didn't," Ben said, "It's Ben."

"This is Ben," Danny said, "He's going to be helping you out in the kitchen."

"Great." Joe said, "I need another pair of hands."

At that moment, a young apprentice chef walked into the kitchen from out the back. He smelled of smoke as he walked past Ben. "And that's Tyler," Danny said, "He's the apprentice chef."

"Is this the new dish pig?" Tyler asked.

"Yes, I'm the new dish pig. Taken your job, have I?" Ben asked.

Tyler pretended that he didn't hear him and walked over to a small sink to wash his hands The tap was operated by a little lever you push with your knee. Danny pointed at two large sinks at the end of the kitchen. There was a pile of dirty cooking utensils beside it, ready to be washed. "There's the sinks," he said, "I'm sure you know what to do. There's a large dishwasher there next to the sinks. Wash them and sanitise them, and then put them away. These guys will tell you where all the stuff goes. It's pretty easy."

"Thanks Danny," Ben said, as he pulled his jacket off and hung it up on a hanger next to a few other jackets. He walked over to the sinks and began to fill up one of them with hot water, and found a container with detergent in it. He poured detergent into the filling sink and it began to froth up. He turned off the tap when it was three quarters full and began to wash the dishes, and then he heard people coming in through the door. Danny poked his head into the kitchen. "It's show time," he said.

Joe walked out the door to the front part of the kitchen, which was set in behind the bar. Tyler stayed out the back preparing food, while Ben washed the dishes. He looked over his shoulder at Tyler and felt a little uncomfortable having his back to him, as he wasn't really sure about him. Tyler glared at him and went back to chopping onions. "First job?" Tyler asked.

"I'm twenty five. I've worked in plenty of places," Ben replied.

"Twenty five?" Tyler remarked, "You don't even look old enough to drink."

"Well, I've been old enough to drink longer than you have," Ben said. He went back to washing dishes, not wanting to engage in any more conversation with Tyler.

"Two slices of bread please," Joe shouted from out the front.

"Coming right up," Tyler said, then muttered under his breath, "You little old cunt."

"You don't like him?" Ben asked.

"He's just such a perfectionist," Tyler said.

"Aren't all chefs?" Ben asked, "In my opinion, they probably should be."

"Who asked you anyway?" Tyler retorted, as he got two slices of bread and passed them through a small window in between the front and rear kitchens. Ben shrugged and continued to wash the dishes. The bar had filled up and the two chefs were running off their feet. The dishes next to Ben grew higher and higher. He kept quiet and washed all the dishes one by one, making sure they were spotless before and after they went in the sanitiser. Eventually, he had no dishes left, and the bar was quiet. He looked around to make sure he hadn't missed anything, and then wiped the bench down and emptied the sink. He dried his hands and walked out to the bar. Danny was polishing off some glasses and putting them in the rack above the bar. "All the dishes are done," Ben said.

"Good job," Danny said, "You want to come in Wednesday through to Saturday for lunch and dinner?"

"Yeah, that would be great. Thanks," Ben said.

He walked back into the kitchen and grabbed his jacket from the hook and threw it around his shoulders. He walked out of the kitchen and pulled up a stool at the bar. Joe came out just behind him and sat with Ben. "Good job today, Ben," Joe said.

"Thanks Joe," Ben replied, "What's the deal with Tyler?"

"Spoilt little brat, in my opinion," Joe said, "Hopefully when he finishes his apprenticeship, he'll find another chef to annoy."

Ben laughed. "If he gives you any cheek, I'll sort him out."

"Just let him be," Joe said, "He's no threat."

Tyler walked through the door from the kitchen. "Good work today, dish pig," he said.

"You too, apprentice chef," Ben said.

"I'll be a qualified chef in six months," Tyler remarked.

"Oh, daddy can't pay for your qualification?" Ben mocked.

"Shut up, dish pig," Tyler said as he walked out.

"I think he likes me," Ben said jokingly.

Joe and Danny both laughed. "You'll fit in perfectly here," Danny said.

EPILOGUE

Six months passed as Ben worked in the kitchen and spent as much time with Alex and William as he could. They had become like a family so quickly, that Ben had almost forgotten what his life as an angel was. He had settled back into human life, and occasionally Marcus would pop into his head. He was still dealing with the grief, but his pain had subsided, and he put all of his energy into his family. Alex knew that one day Ben would have to leave, so she enjoyed it while it lasted. Ben and William became very close, but Alex feared what would happen when Ben had to leave. She didn't want William to be hurt by not having Ben around anymore. Alex understood that Ben couldn't stick around, as everybody would notice that he wouldn't age. It came up in conversation between them every now and then, but they never really got to an answer. Ben found himself more at home than he ever had in his life, and he didn't want to leave.

He woke up one morning and had a quick shower, getting ready to go to work. He walked back into the bedroom and kissed Alex on the forehead, and walked down the stairs and out to his car to drive to the Scottish bar. While he worked, he noticed a small tension between Joe and Tyler. They were snapping at each other, and Tyler was muttering things under his breath when Joe wasn't around. Ben decided to actually try to help him.

"You shouldn't be so nasty towards him. He's taught you everything you know," Ben said.

"You think I care about him? As soon as my apprenticeship finishes, I'm outta here," Tyler said.

"And the only reference you'll have is him. Think about it. You'll never get another job if he is the only referee you've got, and you treat him like this."

"Don't tell me what to do. I work with knives every day and I know how to use them."

"Yeah, you do. You know how to chop food."

Tyler picked up a large knife and threw it at Ben. The world around Ben slowed down, as he had been taught. The knife was coming straight towards him. It was an uneducated throw, and Ben knew he could easily dodge it. He decided to scare Tyler, as he wanted to teach the kid a lesson. He stood completely still as the knife flew through the air towards him. At the last second, his right hand came up in front of his face, and he rotated it counterclockwise. He caught the knife one-handed, by the blade. He put it on the sink and stared at Tyler who was looking at him in awe. "You're not the only one trained how to use knives," Ben said, "The only difference is I've been trained to use them as weapons." He turned around and continued washing dishes. Tyler, seeing that Ben's back was turned, slowly reached for another knife, when suddenly Ben picked up the one that Tyler threw at him, and held it by the blade. He turned around and threw it at the chopping board below Tyler's hand. It spun around with expert precision, and dug into the chopping board right in between Tyler's hand and the knife he was reaching for. "Don't make me prove it."

Ben kept washing the dishes, when Joe walked in. He saw the knife sticking out of the chopping board. "And now you're damaging my chopping boards. What's wrong with you?" he shouted.

Tyler grabbed him and threw him up against the wall. "Listen old man, I don't need you, or this fucking place. Shut the hell up."

Tyler flew backwards across the kitchen and landed against the wall, as Ben had grabbed him by the back of his chef uniform and thrown him across the room, one-handed. Ben's staff appeared in his hand and Joe looked at it in shock. Ben walked over to Tyler and hoisted him up against the wall with the staff. He put the grip of his staff against Tyler's throat and lifted him off the ground with it. "You're right, you don't need this place. I suggest you leave," Ben ordered. He released his grip and Tyler fell back to the ground, before picking himself up and running out the door. Ben let his staff disappear, and Joe walked over to him. "Thank you," he said, "that's all I needed to see."

Ben looked a question at him. "What do you mean?"

"That was my sign. I know who you are now."

"Who am I?" Ben asked calmly.

"You're Marcus' friend. The one who is supposed to take over from him."

"I'm not taking over from Marcus," Ben said, "I'm not that guy anymore."

"Ben, you'll always be that guy. You can't escape it. Now I have to go back to Heaven, because after seeing you, I know that the Great War is coming, and we have to prepare. Eventually, you'll have to come back too."

"Wait, you're an angel?" Ben asked.

"I'm a Cherub," Joe said, "And you're a Seraph, correct?"

"Yeah, but I ain't going back," Ben said.

"You can't stay here," Joe said, "We need the Commander of Battle."

"Yeah well, he's dead."

"Then you must take his place."

"I'm not taking his place," Ben said.

"He would have chosen you, Ben. We can't fight this war without you."

"What the hell! Are you guys everywhere? You're going to have to fight without me. We don't have the sword anymore, and we don't have Marcus anymore. As far as I'm concerned, we've already lost," Ben said.

"I know that you will come to your senses. It's why I was put here, to help you. Now that I've actually found you, I know what it is you seek."

"And what's that?" Ben asked.

"Go back to New York. You will find what you're looking for, there," Joe said.

"And what am I looking for?" Ben asked.

"I think you already know the answer to that, Ben."

Joe flicked something small and silver at the bench. It spun in the air and landed on the stainless steel bench top, continuing to spin. Ben heard the bench top vibrating from the object spinning on it. As it slowed down, he realised it was a ring. He stopped it between his thumb and fore finger, and picked it up. He recognised the etchings on the side. They looked almost tribal and were shaped like wings. It was Marcus' ring. He inspected it closely to make sure it was the same ring. He slid it onto his thumb and looked at Joe with shock in his eyes. "He's alive, isn't he?" Ben asked.

Joe stared at Ben and said nothing. "Tell me!" Ben shouted.

"I honestly don't know. I doubt it. There's no coming back after Purgatory. I just said you will find what you are looking for. Unfortunately, I do know that what you seek, is not Marcus. Go back to New York, Ben."

Ben drove to Alex's house and rushed in the door. He bolted up the stairs and into the lounge room. Alex was sitting on the couch watching TV, and William had his head in her lap. They both looked up at Ben as he came into the room. "You have to leave, don't you?" Alex asked.

Ben slowly nodded. Alex looked down at William and stroked his hair. Ben got down on one knee. "William, come here buddy," Ben whispered. William slowly crawled off the couch and walked sleepily over to Ben. Ben ran his fingers through the boys' hair and ran his hand down the side of his face. He grabbed hold of both his shoulders and looked him in the eyes. "I have to go away, but I'll come back to see you."

William blinked and stared into his fathers' eyes. "Where?"

Ben grabbed William's hand and placed it on his chest. "I'll be right here, son. If you ever need me, just pray really hard and I'll come find you." He wrapped his arms around William and looked over at Alex, who was staring down at the floor. He let go of William and walked over to the couch and sat down next to Alex. "I'll come back," Ben promised.

"This is what I was afraid of Ben," Alex said, "I didn't want William to be hurt by all of this."

"Neither did I, and I promise you I will be back. Every day if I have to. I don't want to miss out on anything!"

Alex reached over and stroked the side of Ben's head. "I know you will. I guess I just wasn't expecting this to happen so soon. We'll be here when you get back. What's happened?"

Ben let out a small sigh. "I don't know. I think maybe Marcus is alive." Ben explained, "And if he is, I have to find him. There is a war coming and we can't fight it without him."

"I understand," Alex whispered.

Ben kissed her and stood up to walk out. He stroked William's hair as he walked past him, and then turned to look at the two of them before leaving. A small tear fell from his eye as he turned and walked down the stairs and out to his car. He drove the car back to his parents' house and told them he was leaving. He said his goodbyes and transported to his house in New York. It looked like it hadn't been touched. He tried to turn on the light, but nothing happened. He picked up the phone and heard no dial tone. He walked out the front door and stood in the morning daylight and stretched. He felt as though his purpose as an angel was beginning all over again. He decided to fix up his house as he hadn't done so after the demon smashed through the window, and the grey cement-like puddles were still on the carpet.

Ben walked to an ATM and pulled out his bank card, pushing it into the slot. He hadn't actually checked the balance since before Marcus died, so he figured he'd see how much was actually in there. He stepped back in shock when he read the receipt. There was over two hundred thousand dollars in there. He figured it must be a mistake, until he remembered Marcus telling him to check his bank balance. He realised that he hadn't checked it since Marcus had said that. This must be what Marcus was talking about. He withdrew a few hundred dollars and then got the electricity and phone reconnected back at his house. He then made some phone calls about a new window, and a new carpet. He figured that if he was going to base his operations there, he had to make it habitable. Once the window and carpet were fixed, he figured he would start at Murphy's. He walked in through the door under the neon light, and up to the bar. He sat down on a stool and waited to be served. Mike came up to him instantly. "Ben," Mike said, "I haven't seen you here in months! Where have you been?"

"I've been in Huntington," Ben said.

"Oh, well welcome back. You able to fix up your tab anytime soon?"

"I suppose so," Ben said.

He pulled out his wallet, and pulled out two hundred dollars and handed it to Mike. "Keep the change," he said, "and pour me a drink while you're at it."

"Cheers," Mike said, "Where's Marcus?"

"Haven't seen him," Ben said, "Have you?"

"Not since last time he was here with you and Luke. You don't see him anymore?"

"Not really. He kind of disappeared. We're not sure where to find him," Ben explained.

"Well, if he turns up here, I'll let him know you're trying to find him. I hope everything's okay between you two."

"Everything is fine," Ben said.

Mike poured Ben a scotch and sat it in front of him. He took a long sip of the drink and looked around the room. He didn't see any familiar faces and he felt like a bit of a wanderer, even though this was his regular bar. He quickly finished his drink and left the glass on the bar. "Thanks Mike."

Mike waved at him as he left. He figured he'd try his second option. He walked past his house and made his way to the strip club where he met Gabriel. He walked in the door and was stopped with a hand on his chest. "Can I help you?" the man just inside the doorway asked.

"I'm here to see Gabriel," Ben said.

"Gabriel isn't here anymore," the man said.

Ben stared into the man's eyes. He tried to see if he could read them. "Are you lying to me?" Ben asked.
The man shook his head. Ben didn't see any sign of aggression in the man's eyes, but more of a content,

apologetic look. Ben nodded. "Any idea where he went?" Ben asked.

"No idea, I'm afraid. I'm sorry Ben."

Ben looked up at the man. "How did you know my name? We never told you when we came here that time."

"Everyone knows about you, Ben," the man said.

"Right," Ben said as he left. He wandered down the street and back to his house. He walked in and made his way to his bedroom and slumped himself down on the bed, and fell asleep instantly.

When Ben woke up, he felt a little more of a weight pulling down on him. He felt depressed and as if he couldn't succeed. He continually tried to think like Marcus and wondered what he would do in this situation. All he could come back to was the fact that Marcus spent one hundred years searching for his sword, and then gave up and eventually found it six hundred years later. Ben felt like he didn't have that much time before the war started, and he began to stress. He spent countless hours, days, weeks, and months reading the bible and researching all he could, trying to figure out if there was any kind of small clue that would help him to actually understand what Joe had meant by telling him to go back to New York. Joe never actually confirmed that Marcus was alive; he just told him to go back to New York. Now that Ben was in New York, he had no idea what to do next.

Ben was surprised at how much he found on the internet about angels was actually accurate. Of course, Wikipedia is written by its users, so obviously some beings that actually knew the truth had made a few contributions. He learnt as much as he could to try to better understand everything as a whole. He began to buy a bottle of scotch every night and sit at home studying, hoping to find some sort of answer that would lead him to find whatever it was that Joe had told him to come back to New York for. He gave up on the idea that Marcus was still alive. He figured it couldn't be possible. He began to believe that he was supposed to take Marcus' place and become the Commander of Battle himself. *The angel will fall and rise again.* He started to think of that statement as himself. He had fallen, and was feeling that he would rise again to take up the position that was being offered to him.

The Revelation became a destiny that he seemed destined to fulfil. He didn't quite understand it, but knew it had something to do with him. A sudden thought hit him. The entire time he had been researching and reading, he hadn't once been to Marcus' apartment. He remembered the books on the bookshelf; his whole life on earth, that he'd written into journals - all except one. He transported into Marcus' living room and looked around. It had felt like forever since he'd been there. Nothing had changed, although he noticed a small blinking light coming from the entrance hallway; one he hadn't noticed before, because every time he was there, the alarm wasn't on, and therefore, the light on the keypad wasn't blinking. He remembered Marcus talking about the sprinkler system being hooked up to the alarm and rushed over to the keypad. He didn't want the books to be destroyed by the water, so he looked at the keypad, hoping it would will him to know the code. He thought back through the times he'd spent with Marcus, knowing his habits, knowing all his little obsessive compulsive traits. A number hit him. He punched in the four digits on the keypad. Two tones sounded from the keypad and the blinking light stopped. He silently congratulated himself for knowing Marcus well enough that he could guess. Although Marcus was smart, he wasn't fond of committing things to memory, so the apartment number twice would be easy to remember; not to mention that he had some fascination with the number twenty three.

Ben didn't give it another thought and stepped over to the bookshelf. He remembered seeing Marcus turn it around, as it was a rotating bookshelf. Ben pushed one side of it, and it spun around as he'd seen it do before. The journals all lay in front of him as he braced himself to begin. But, where to begin? He read through all the spines as they boasted many different times throughout history. Ben was aghast at some of the titles. Both World Wars, and many others that followed, as well as previous wars. His eyes glanced over the spine of the book about piracy, as his curiosity lingered. But, he wanted to be able to read them chronologically. He wanted to start at the beginning. But, which one was the beginning?

Ben scanned through the spines, past a book, where the spine read 'Camelot'. He disregarded it quickly, and found the gap where the Downfall book was supposed to be. Out of all the books on the shelf, that would be the one he wanted to read most. If only it were there. He moved past the gap and landed on Ethiopia. A memory stirred. He remembered Marcus talking about carrying the Ark of the Covenant to Ethiopia. He had said God had asked him to take it out of Jerusalem and that it would be safe there. That had to be the first book. He pulled it down off the shelf and opened it, only to find an ornate key with a post it note. The note was addressed to him. He was suddenly confused. How did Marcus know he'd pick that book? Why did Marcus even leave him a note in one of the journals? Because Marcus knew he wouldn't be there. Marcus knew he was going to die. The realisation hit Ben hard. Marcus had known and he hadn't said anything. He just left this note, which said something about a blade that takes back, annuls, revokes. And then there was something written in Hebrew. Ben understood the word, as angels speak universally. He spoke the word aloud, "Aron".

He was confused. "What does Ark have to do with it? Does he mean the Ark of the Covenant?"

Ben thought for a moment longer, repeating the word. "Aron, Aron, Aron..." It hit him. "It means Ark." It was the word Arus had left on the wall of the cave in Chislehurst. The one that glowed occasionally; pronounced 'ARON'. Arus had told the curator of the caves that Marcus would mention his name, and called himself Aron. Arus knew something. But where would he find Arus? Or worse, how would Arus react to him trying to find him? They didn't exactly part on the best of terms. The only time Ben and Arus actually spoke, Ben called him a coward. Arus wasn't too fond of that, but he let it slide for the time being. Ben looked at the book about Ethiopia. He could figure it out. Marcus had left it there for him, so it was up to him. He sat down on the couch and began to read. He learnt all about the Chapel of the Tablet, where the guardian resided with the Ark of the Covenant. The chapel was built when Marcus was there, and he had a hand in the design of the place. He also referred to himself as Suriel. Ben stopped to think on that for a second. "Suriel must be his real name. He changed it to Marcus to adapt to humanity," he said out loud. He knew Marcus must have been a pseudonym. He continued reading. Toward the end of the book, Ben was made aware of a chamber beneath the chapel; a place that only Marcus could enter, only accessed by a key placed into a stone shaped like a chest. A library. It was at the rear of the chapel, and there was a warning to all who would read, only the truest of good may walk the ground. Beware.

Ben closed the book and looked at the key, with the note. He walked over to the computer and fired it up. Whilst he waited for it to load, he went to the kitchen to make himself a drink. He didn't think Marcus would have minded that he help himself. He found some scotch, and poured a glass, neat, as he sat down at the computer. He opened up the search and typed in *Chapel of the Tablet, Ethiopia*. The browser came up with many pages, but he wanted pictures. He found the pictures tab and scrolled through until he found one he liked. It was a good view of the chapel, with trees surrounding it. Marcus had told him that transporting was possible if one hadn't been there before, but just by thinking about the place. He had an image, and he believed he could do it. He closed his eyes and concentrated, hard. A slight breeze hit his face as he opened his eyes and found himself standing exactly where he had imagined; within the trees, along the side of the chapel. He looked around at his surroundings and made sure he still had the book, the key, and the note in his hands. He set out to walk around the back and found the stone on the ground, resembling a chest, with a small key shaped hole in the front. He placed the key in the lock, and turned it. The ground started to vibrate as he removed the key, and saw the stone part in front of him as a staircase appeared, which led down under the chapel. He reluctantly receded down the stairs and came to a wall. There was writing on the wall in a language he didn't understand, but he loved puzzles. He stared at the phrase on the wall, knowing he could figure it out. All he needed to do was work out one word, as there were recurring letters. Five words; two recurring words. The first word was obviously an adverb. It was the same as the fourth word. He focused on the second word. "Five letters, with double letters. It's either O, E, L, or S. Maybe T. Can't be A, can't be I, can't be U."

Ben focused on the third word, which had two letters, the first of which was the same as the double letters in the second word. "That rules out E and L. Unless it's in French. Doubtful."

He looked closer. "Gotta be O." He started going through the five letter words he knew with double O. "Proof, Sloop, Shoot, Spoon, Flood, Blood..." He stopped. "Blood."

He looked at the last word; it had the two of the same letters. If the first word were Blood, the last word started with L, and ended in B. "Lamb."

He stepped back and looked at the whole phrase. "The Blood of the Lamb. Has to be. Lamb of God was Jesus Christ, Blood of the Lamb would be the blood of Jesus."

Nothing happened. Ben looked down at the note. *A blade that takes back, annuls, revokes.* A blade with the blood of Christ. Ben vaguely remembered hearing about a spear that had stabbed Jesus in his side, as he hung on the cross. "The Spear of Destiny," he said.

Nothing happened. It was the only thing he knew that fit. He realised he needed help. He would need to find Arus. Unless, Lucifer knew something? Ben turned around and walked back up the stairs to the outside. The stone began rumbling again as it closed. He turned to watch it. "I gotta learn how to make this shit," he said to himself

He transported himself instantly into Lucifer's house in Hell, right onto the three curved steps surrounding his throne. Lucifer was sitting there, mid conversation with someone in the chair in the middle of the room. They both stopped and looked as Ben appeared, and gave an abashed smile. He put his hand on Lucifer's arm and turned to face the person sitting in the chair in the middle. "Sorry, this will only take a minute. I need to borrow him."

Ben closed his eyes to transport them both to Ethiopia. Nothing happened. Ben opened his eyes and looked up at Lucifer, who looked at him bewildered. They were still in Hell. Ben closed his eyes and tried again, this time placing two hands on Lucifer's arm. Nothing happened. He opened his eyes and looked back at Lucifer with confusion. "You're resisting," he said.

"Yes."

Ben thought for a second. "We can do that?"

Lucifer nodded. "Yes, we can."

Ben gave a head tilt with a shrug of acceptance. "I need you to come with me, now."

Lucifer looked at his guest. "I'm very sorry, this doesn't normally happen." He turned back to Ben. "Can't you see I'm busy?"

Ben had no choice. "I found Marcus' secret library."

Lucifer raised his eyebrows as he turned back to his guest. "My apologies, I'm afraid I have to reschedule."

"What?" the man shrieked.

"I'm sorry, pressing matters," Lucifer remarked.

"This is pressing! I need your help! They're gonna kill me!"

Lucifer smiled, "In which case, you'll end up here. We'll talk then". Lucifer stood up and shook Ben's hands off his arm. "How's the 14th for you?" Lucifer waved his hand and the man disappeared.

Ben looked a question at him. "That sounded kind of important."

"Eh, I don't really care for people who come calling for financial gain."

"So people actually do come to sell their soul? So you are the devil!"

Lucifer smirked. "Don't tell anyone. Let's go."

Ben grabbed Lucifer's arm and they found themselves in Ethiopia, just next to the stone. Ben pulled out the key and put it in the hole like he had earlier. They both heard the rumble as the stone parted again, revealing the staircase. Lucifer looked around to get his bearings. "Ethiopia?" he asked. Ben nodded.

They walked down the staircase and came to the wall again with the inscription. Lucifer looked at it intently, but with confusion. "Well that doesn't make sense."

"What doesn't?" Ben asked.

"It's in Enochian."

"Whatever that is."

"It's a language that was created by humans. They believed it to be the language of the angels. They were wrong."

"That explains why I couldn't read it."

"It says..."

"The Blood of the Lamb, I already figured that out," Ben said.

Lucifer looked at him. "How? You just said you couldn't read it."

Ben shifted his weight to his other foot. "I like puzzles. Double letters in the second word, two letter word starting with that same letter, had to be O. Figured it was Blood, which made the last word Lamb. Seemed fitting. The Blood of the Lamb, Lamb of God."

"The Blood of Christ," Lucifer said.

Ben nodded, "That's what I gathered".

Lucifer looked closer at the wall; not at the Enochian inscription, but at the other carvings surrounding it. There were five, and they all symbolised five different things that Lucifer knew instantly. He placed his finger on each of them as he said them aloud. "War..." He moved his finger to the next. "Famine..." The next, "Pestilence...", "Death..."

He stopped on the last one. It was dead centre and directly below the Enochian inscription. "Conquest..."

Ben stepped forward. "The horsemen?" Lucifer nodded. "Marcus said there were five."

Lucifer nodded again. "There was. Conquest was the first, and the strongest. I think I know where this is heading."

"Please, enlighten me!" Ben said.

Lucifer stood up and looked at the phrase again. "A weapon imbued with the Blood of the Lamb is the only thing that could kill the horsemen. Since the Lamb of God was the one to open the seals of the Apocalypse, his blood was the key to it."

Ben nodded, "The Spear of Destiny".

Lucifer looked at Ben. "Yes." Lucifer looked back at the wall. "But it was destroyed."

"Why?" Ben asked.

"Many reasons. It's an old tale, one that has been told many times, many different ways." He stood face on to Ben. "You would know it as the Legend of King Arthur."

Ben almost fell over in shock. "There was a book on Marcus' bookshelf in his apartment! It said 'Camelot'. It didn't even register."

"Probably not relevant to the library. But the Spear of Destiny, well, that seems to be."

"How so?"

Lucifer sat on the steps. He sat in thought for a moment to try to remember all the details. "What do you think Excalibur was?"

"It was the sword in the stone. Everybody knows that," Ben said.

"But originally, it wasn't a sword. It was a spear."

"Excalibur was the Spear of Destiny?"

Lucifer nodded again, "Arus fashioned it into a sword".

"Wait, Arus was there?"

"He was Merlin."

Ben was full of questions. He couldn't believe what he was hearing. "I've met Merlin?"

"Yes, you've met Morgan Le Fay, too."

Ben opened his eyes wide. He couldn't think of who he had met that would be Morgan Le Fay. Then it suddenly dawned on him. "Eligos." Lucifer nodded in agreement. They sat in silence for a long moment until Ben remembered the note Marcus had left him. He pulled it from his pocket and read it again, then handed it to Lucifer. "Marcus left me a clue."

Lucifer gave Ben a disgruntled look. "You could have lead with that. Let me take a look."

He read the note aloud. "*A blade, that takes back, that annuls, revokes.*" He paused, and a memory stirred. "No, it's a myth... It doesn't exist."

Ben stepped forward with intrigue. "What's a myth? What doesn't exist?"

Lucifer stood up and looked at the wall. "The Rescinder Blade." The wall began to rumble as a gap formed in the centre. The two sides parted with immense vibration as they both watched in awe, and the library revealed itself. Lucifer looked in shock. "It exists... What have you done, Marcus?"

Ben looked at Lucifer. "What do you mean?"

Lucifer almost gulped. "Of course, he would know something about it."

They saw bookshelves and bookshelves, and more bookshelves, as well as a few desks, with an assortment of items on them, and chests. Not to mention weapons; piles and piles of weapons. Ben's eyes were drawn to the two Colt Dragoons sitting on a shelf above a desk full of bullets. Black with chrome trim. Immaculate. "What are those?"

Lucifer looked up at the guns Ben was pointing to. He nodded with the same admiration. "Those are Marcus' pistols. Deadly. One kills demons, the other kills angels."

Ben stepped back in shock. "Kills angels? Why?"

Lucifer smirked. "Can't trust anyone. Why do you think even angels feared him?"

Ben nodded. He could understand that completely. His eyes roamed around all the shelves until they finally settled on the shelf right in front of him. Something about it was familiar. They were journals; handwritten journals, all in alphabetical order, and they were all the same as the ones in Marcus' apartment. There was only one difference. The missing book from the apartment, wasn't missing from this shelf. Ben stepped forward and read the spine. "Downfall," he whispered.

He pulled the journal from the shelf and looked at it closely, almost afraid to open it as he looked up at Lucifer. "Lucifer," he said. Lucifer walked over to him. He had been wandering around looking intently at everything there, trying to find anything of significance. He noticed the journal in Ben's hand and stepped closer. Ben held up the book, revealing the name on the spine. Hand carved, and filled in with gold. "Downfall," Ben said again.

Lucifer opened his eyes wide and looked at Ben. He hadn't seen him in close to a year, then all of a sudden he popped up out of nowhere and whisked them away to Marcus' secret library, that only opened by speaking the name of a weapon that wasn't supposed to exist, that Lucifer thought was only a myth. Marcus knew something about it. Lucifer breathed out a sigh, "Ben, the Rescinder Blade exists".

Ben lowered the book and looked a question at Lucifer. "What is the Rescinder Blade?"

Lucifer sat down in the chair by the desk with all the bullets on it. "Back in the time of King Arthur, Arus was tasked with disarming the horsemen, as Conquest had become too powerful. He was serving his purpose; to conquer. So armed with the Spear, and the army of King Arthur, they hunted him and the others. They disarmed all of the horsemen, taking their powerful belongings, and King Arthur, wielding the Spear of Destiny, now a sword named Excalibur, killed Conquest. But, killing a horseman unleashes their essence, and it spreads to the closest living thing, or things. That just happened to be Arthur. All of a sudden, Arthur began conquering. But Conquest wasn't dead. No, you can't kill the horsemen. He resurfaced, a powerless husk, destined to reclaim his essence. He took a human form, known as Mordred. He reclaimed his essence, only to become stronger than before; stronger than anything we've ever come across.

"So began the fall of Arthur, and God and Arus banished Conquest to the abyss. The Spear of Destiny was destroyed, to ensure no being had the power to kill or control the horsemen. For, if they were to reunite with their essence after death, they would all become stronger. After Conquest was banished, the remaining horsemen just disappeared. Nobody heard a peep from them. Then, a myth started to circulate. One of the confiscated belongings of the horsemen had been fashioned into a weapon. A blade, crafted from the melted down steel of the very sword that belonged to War."

Ben opened his eyes wide. "The horseman? War?"

"The horseman. It was supposedly imbued with the Blood of the Lamb. Using a weapon of a horseman, and the Blood of Christ, one could create a weapon that could essentially kill anything; even God. Hence, why it was just a myth. No one believed it could be real. Who would do something so stupid?"

Ben held up the book of Downfall. "Let's find out, shall we?"

To be concluded...

ABOUT THE AUTHOR

Beginning a lifetime of music at the young age of four, singing for family and friends, Matt found he had caught the music bug. He furthered his talents, first learning to play the guitar at the age of eight. Matt formed many bands over the years, playing in many venues across Victoria and interstate.

After the death of his brother in 2005, Matt took a large break from playing gigs and began writing his first novel, Sword of the Angels. The story quickly developed into a trilogy, which gave him an outlet for his grief; allowing him to create characters and situations for the memory of his brother to live on.

The Revelation Trilogy is a fictional novel about the struggle of balance between good and evil, with friendship, adventure, betrayal, war, and unlikely alliances.

www.whitelightshop.com